THE YOUNGEST SON

THE TRENGROUSE BALL
BOOK TWO

ELIZABETH LEYDIN

IMPROBABLE FICTIONS

ISBN 978-1-7635241-4-9

Improbable Fictions
PO Box 283
Annandale NSW 2038
Australia
contact@improbablefictions.com

THE TRENGROUSE BALL

The Trengrouse Ball…one magic night in a Cornish summer. Music, dancing, flirting and laughter. And deception, abduction, love and loss. New attractions, new hopes, and old flames rekindled. For some, a culmination. For others, a new beginning.

The Trengrouse Ball series follows the lives and loves of the Trengrouse family: eight grown children of the Earl of Trengrouse, each of whom is searching for the life they need; each battling their own fears but hoping for happy ever after.

After the Trengrouse Ball, their lives will never be the same again…

CHAPTER 1

"The Earl of Westholm, now he *would* be a catch! Make sure you take his attention." Mama lowered her voice, but Katie wished it was *much* lower. Mama's voice was so penetrating. She rubbed her brow where she could feel a headache forming.

"He's dancing with Melissa Trengrouse, Mama. He's not going to look at me, after her." Melissa was the diamond in the Trengrouse family. Tall and beautifully formed, with a face that could launch ships. A contrast to Katie's own average height and merely pretty features.

"She's such a bluestocking. They say she even speaks Ancient Greek!" Mama dismissed Melissa with a sniff. "Gentlemen prefer *domestic* women. Now, don't spend your time dancing with the Trengrouse boys. That's no better than dancing with your brothers."

Katie smiled. It was true that the "Trengrouse boys", all five of them, had always treated her more or less as a sister. A footman went past with glasses on a silver tray. The silver winked in the candlelight and a stab of pain went through her skull, right behind her left eye. Oh, no. Not a megrim. Not now!

"May I have the honour?" Marcus Hindock, one of her brother Denzell's friends. A nice boy, but pockets to let, as Den might say. Her mother sighed far too audibly but waved her onto the dance floor. Katie knew what she was thinking: Better to be dancing with a nobody than look like a wallflower.

The Trengrouse Ball was this year's summer gala. Her friend Kerenza Trengrouse's 18th birthday ball, and all of Cornwall, and quite a few nobles and gentry from further afield, were in attendance.

Her mother had been cock-a-hoop over it, as it would give Katie some "town acquaintances" before their planned London Season later in the year.

As they took hands and skipped down their set in a country dance, Katie could admire the elegant ballroom, the lavish use of wax candles, the elegance and gleam of the women's dresses. The rich scent of the masses of lilies, however, was making her headache worse.

If it continued, she was going to be in real trouble.

The dance ended and Marcus escorted her back to her mother, where another young man was waiting. One of Mama's picks, this, no doubt at all. A dazzling specimen with impeccable black satin knee breeches and a sapphire pin in his neckcloth.

"Katherine, may I present Viscount Ardlesh. My lord, my daughter Katherine."

Katie curtseyed beautifully and Mama smiled. Viscount Ardlesh was the eldest son of the Earl of Glasfar, on the Scottish side of the border. A rich and well established family—but so far from home!

She hated having to assess every man she met in terms of his suitability as a husband, but that was the reality of being on the Marriage Mart, which she would be as soon as she reached London.

"May I have the honour?" the Viscount said. He couldn't have *not* said it in the circumstances, but he wouldn't have approached Mama if he hadn't wanted to dance with her, so at least she could smile at him with real friendliness.

It was a waltz next—quite dashing of the Trengrouses!—and it was quite strange to be held so firmly by a man she didn't know. The Viscount was punctiliously correct, keeping her at the proper distance, discussing trivialities. He seemed quite concerned about the new trend for military-style jackets, and expected her to have an opinion about it.

As her Mama's well-trained daughter, her opinion was naturally the same as his, and his look of calm complacency deepened.

She was bored before the dance was half over, but she knew not to show it. Her headache was getting worse; lights danced in front of her eyes and the strange metallic taste which foretold a bad megrim was in her moth.

IVES TRENGROUSE CONSIDERED RESCUING Kitty-kat from that nincompoop she was dancing with. Ardlesh was a notable bore. But the next dance would be a long country dance, and he couldn't be in that when he might need to be off in an instant.

He had his scouts both inside and outside. Inside, footmen. Outside, smugglers. Ready for anything.

"What are you grinning at?" Melissa came up behind him and stood by his side.

"Nothing, Twin. Nothing you need be concerned about."

"Another scrape? Just don't ruin Keri's party."

"Never fear." He grinned at her.

"Mama says it's time for me to think about marriage," Melissa said. "I don't think it's at all fair that she's not saying the same to you."

"Men get a few more years." Ives acknowledged it wasn't fair with his tone, and then remembered it was Melissa he was speaking to, and said it out loud. She was renowned in the family for misunderstanding people's meaning, or missing the point of jokes altogether. Ivory tower thinking, her father called it. Shame she wasn't a man—she'd have made a perfect Oxford don. "It's *not* fair."

She nodded, satisfied. "If I have to marry, you should too."

"Heaven forfend!" He threw up a hand as though parrying a blow, and she laughed, which made him happy. It was good to hear his twin laugh. "I'm not the marrying kind, I don't think."

"I'm not either, but *I* don't get a choice."

"If you truly were strongly against it, I don't think Mama *or* Papa would force it."

"They want me to have *children!*" She shuddered, and he grinned again. Melissa's aversion to children was well known.

He'd make sure she was all right. If she didn't marry, she could come and live with him at Kirwich. Sooner or later he'd need to move there, and Melissa could too. She'd like Kirwich; it was quiet and had a good library.

She went off with a light step and he shrugged. She was so beautiful, the likelihood of her being an old maid was none. He thanked God that no one forced noblemen into marriage anymore, as they had in medieval times. Of course, he'd have to bite the bullet eventually. That was what one did. But later. Much, much later. When he was thirty, perhaps.

. . .

KATIE PUT a handkerchief to her mouth and hurried out of the ballroom. If she could just get to the ladies withdrawing-room in time…

Sally-Ann was the attendant maid; as soon as Katie came into view she grabbed the hand-washing bowl and held it out. Thank God for maids who'd known you since you were tiny. Sally-Ann was her best friend's maid; Kerenza and Sally-Ann had seen her sick with a *megrim* so many times, it was barely worth a raised eyebrow.

Lud, how she *hated* vomiting.

"There. You'll be right as rain now," Sally-Ann said kindly, handing her a cool flannel to wipe her face and hands with.

The candle flames still stabbed at her eyes, but she knew that what she needed now was to go home and sleep it off. Then she really would be right as rain. She sank down on an armchair and covered her eyes.

"I'll get Mr Denzell." Sally-Ann sailed out of the room, carrying the covered basin. Yes. Getting her brother was a good idea.

Much better than summoning her mother. Den would sort out her leaving the party early.

It was *so* disappointing! Kerenza's eighteenth birthday ball had been the highlight of the summer in this little corner of Cornwall, and she was going to miss half of it. Her mother…Katie shuddered. Her mother would *not* be pleased. There were at least a dozen gentlemen Mama had planned to introduce her to, and they had only managed three so far, not counting Marcus Hindock.

A tap came on the door. "Kit? Are you all right? I can't really come in there."

Katie dragged herself out of the chair and opened the door. The music from the ballroom swept in; a spike of pain hit her behind her eye and went right up to her skull.

"You poor poppet," Den said. "I've sent for my carriage. It'll take you home and then come back for Mama and I – unless you'd like me to go with you?"

He didn't sound enthusiastic about that, and why would he? He knew well enough that she'd simply fall asleep in the carriage. She always did after she'd vomited.

"No, of course not. John Coachman will take me home safely."

Den's carriage was significantly more comfortable than their mother's, which was why Mama had commandeered it for tonight. He used it for regular trips to London; like the Trengrouse boys, he had business interests there.

"Bless you." He dropped a kiss on her brow and shepherded her towards the side entrance. "I told John to bring the coach around to the side. Less fuss."

"*Thank* you!" In their private sibling vocabulary, "fuss" was code for their mother kicking up a stink. She would probably insist on Katie staying, even if enduring heat and candle-flames and music and *smiling* at people meant another bout of vomiting. Dancing would be impossible, but Mama believed you could will yourself not to be sick, and said so. Frequently.

The coach was there, John Coachman

solid and familiar on the perch. It might be Den's carriage, but John let no one else drive the Kelynack women.

Katie climbed in and settled back on the seat with relief. It was so nice and *dark* in here. Even the light of the full moon, drenching the landscape with silver, was too much at the moment.

She could feel herself falling asleep before they'd even made it past the Trengrouse Hall gateposts.

"Sɪʀ! Mr Denzell's coachman's been called."

Ives Trengrouse grinned and clapped the footman on the shoulder. "Good man, Bryok."

Now to make his escape from the ballroom without either parent noticing. He'd been waiting for this opportunity for a month, even since Den had abandoned him on a tidal island in the cove and he'd had to swim to shore, his clothes tied around his neck. The salt water had ruined a good jacket, and his boots had never been the same.

He slid out onto the terrace and ran for the stables. It would take the Kelynack coachman a minute or two to put the horses to, and his own mare was waiting, ready saddled. He and his men, Gus and Benesek, would be out on the road well before that coach.

It was early for Den to leave, but then he'd never liked parties that much. So much the better. Ives grinned again. With any luck, he'd be done with this business and back at the ball before anyone noticed he'd gone.

IVES PULLED up a kerchief over his nose and mouth, smiling. Here it came. He waved to Gus and Benesek and they took up positions behind the aspens across the road. They were only a mile or so from Trengrouse Hall, but it was a deserted stretch of road and there were no buildings overlooking this bend.

His mare moved under him uneasily, and he patted her and whispered, "Steady on, old girl."

The coach lumbered up the slight hill towards the copse he was hiding in. The moon was lowering, but it showed the arms on the door clearly enough. Besides, he'd know those chestnuts anywhere. It was Den's coach. Time for revenge.

He urged the mare out onto the road.

"Stand and deliver!"

The coach pulled up, the horses showing the whites of their eyes. Gus and Benesek were up on the box in a trice, and had bundled the coachman down, tied and gagged before he could let out more than a cry of protest. There were benefits to hiring smugglers as your right hand men. They were efficient.

"Gently, lads," Ives said. "Tie him loosely, so he can get home before dawn."

At the sound of his voice, the coachman stopped struggling and peered up at him. "Aye, it's me," Ives said. "No need to worry about your master." Oddly, the man wasn't reassured and tried to shout through his gag. John, wasn't it? "Dinnae squall, John, he deserves it."

Den hadn't poked his head out yet, which was strange. Ives reached for the coach's door handle and heard, as clear as day, gentle snores coming from the occupant. He laughed softly. So much the better. If Den had taken too much drink, even easier to drive him to an isolated place and abandon him to make his own way back, just as Den had abandoned him.

Gus was on the box of the coach and his horse was tied behind.

Ives gave a tip of the head and led off down the road. There was a deserted farmhouse about five miles away. They should make it before the moon set. He whistled *Sally Lunn* as they went. He'd miss the rest of Keri's ball, but it would be worth it when he saw Den's face.

. . .

JOHN LYNDER STRUGGLED free of the last loop of rope and wrenched the gag out of his mouth. He set off down the hill, running as fast as he could, back to Trengrouse Hall.

Mr Den would have to sort this mishmash out.

At least she was with Mr Ives. A rapscallion, prone to roaming around with smugglers, but a good-hearted lad.

It was only a mile or so but he wasn't used to running, and came up to the house wheezing and gulping air. The front door was open and he followed the path of light up the steps. Carveth the butler stepped in front of him, all forbidding majesty, and then recognised him.

"Lynder?"

"Get Mr Denzell!" John gasped.

THIS WAS THE MOMENT. Ives grinned at Gus, who held the horses at the head. Gus gave a thumbs up. He was the son of the local smuggler boss, and the two of them had been partners in mischief since they were knee high—four of them, really, because Den had always been part of it, and so had his brother Petroc before he joined the Army.

"Wake 'im up fast and noisy," Gus hissed. Good idea. Barely stopping himself from laughing out loud, Ives grabbed the handle of the coach door and ripped the door open.

"Yo-ho-ho!" he yelled.

Someone screamed. A girl. Den had a *girl* in there with him? Yo ho very ho! This would be good.

Ives stuck his head in the doorway. The interior was dim, but the coach sidelight must have shown his own face clearly.

"I-Ives?"

A tremulous, high voice. And deucedly familiar.

"Kitty?" Damnation. Den was nowhere to be seen. Just Katherine Kelynack, Den's little sister. What the devil?

"What's happening?" Kitty sat up straighter and leaned forward, peering out. "Where are we?"

"At Treford Farm."

"But–" Her voice sharpened. "Is this another one of your stupid jokes?"

She shifted forward and he instinctively moved to swing her down to the road.

The setting moon illuminated a pale face with a rather tremulous mouth. Poor lamb. She must have had a shock when he shouted at her. "Why did you want to play a prank on *me*?"

"I didn't!" She ought to know better than that. "I thought you were Den! I mean, what are you doing in Den's carriage? You're supposed to be at the ball!"

"Don't you get huffy at *me*, Ives Trengrouse! I had the megrim and Den sent me home to sleep it off." She put her hand to her mouth. "I've already been sick once."

"Oh." Yes. That explained it all. Kitty-kat's headaches were legendary. "Are you all right?"

"Well, yes, but home is ten miles in the other direction! We'll never get there before the moon sets."

The beat of a horse's hooves came to them across the still night, and a familiar figure came into view around the bend of the road. He'd know that grey gelding anywhere. It was *his*. And he'd deliberately not used it tonight because it was so recognisable.

Denzell. The hide of the fellow, taking Ives' own horse. And worse, riding him well!

Den came up to them in silence, and swung down from the grey. He looked unusually stern.

Den! Oh, thank goodness. He would sort out this mess.

"I should call you out for this," he hissed to Ives. Katie gulped. Was she in trouble too?

"What?" Ives put up his hands. "It was a joke. To get you back for abandoning me on that island."

"It's one thing to get back at me. But to involve my *sister*–"

"Hold on there, matey! I didn't know it was Kitty. It was *your* coach! I thought you were shabbing off early because Melza gave you the cold shoulder."

Oh, that was interesting. She hadn't realised that Denzell had a *tendre* for Demelza, Ives' sister. That explained a great deal of the past month.

Denzell bit back a reply—probably a swear word. "You've made a muff of it, Ives."

"No harm done," Ives said, as lighthearted as always now Den wasn't hissing at him. "You can take the girl home and all's well."

"All is *not* well!" Den turned to her and took her hands. "I'm sorry, my dear. But too many people know that you'd left the ball. They asked after you and I explained I'd sent you home. And too many people saw John Coachman stagger up and ask for me, and me rushing off."

Katie stood there for a moment, the blood draining down to her feet. Her skin was clammy, her head light.

"I'm ruined." Every debutante's nightmare. She had been alone with Ives Trengrouse for several hours. There wasn't a gossiping matron this side of John O'Groats who wouldn't believe the worst.

"No, no, not *ruined*. Just…"

"Compromised," she whispered.

"But–" Ives' voice was shaky; the first time she'd ever heard him anything other than confident.

"No buts, Ives. The two of you will have to marry."

Katie fainted.

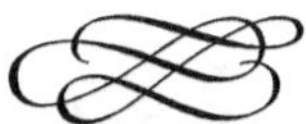

CHAPTER 2

*M*arried. The idea was like being swept off his feet in a strong current, being pulled out to a stormy sea with no hope of rescue.

Married.

He helped Den manoeuvre Katie into the coach and laid her on the seat. She'd taken it hard. Couldn't help but feel a tad piqued. Was marrying him *so* bad? Even the thought made his guts clench and his palms sweat. He was only twenty, for God's sake! If he'd thought of marriage, it was in the far future.

Smoothing back a strand of Kitten's hair,

he sighed. Couldn't let Kitty-kat down. That termagant of a mother would shred her to pieces if they went back now. As her husband, he could protect her from that folderol.

And if he had to get married, better to marry someone he knew and liked. Wasn't it?

SHE CAME AWAKE in the darkness of the coach. The door was open, and Ives and Den were discussing her just outside.

"I'm *not* going to Gretna Green!" Ives said in a low voice. "It's a ridiculous idea. We can just go back and announce that we're engaged. We can fudge the timing and say you caught up with us almost at once."

"No one will believe that. But I suppose an engagement would kill most of the gossip."

Most. No, that wasn't good enough.

"Absolutely not." She pulled herself to the door of the coach and Den helped her down the steps—at least they'd had the sense to put the steps *down* this time. As often happened after a headache, everything looked too bright, and seemed unreal, as though it were all a dream. Perhaps it was! Perhaps she was still asleep. She prayed that was true.

But when her foot hit the rough surface of the road and she felt gravel through the thin sole of her dancing slippers, she knew she was wide awake. Her heart clenched with dismay. Married! *Married*! What would Mama say? What would she say if they *didn't* marry?

"Gretna Green is a madcap idea!" Ives ran a hand through his hair distractedly. "It's a good ten days' travel! Maybe more."

"I'll come with you,' Den said. 'Chaperone."

"And pay with what? It's three weeks until quarter day, and I don't have half the blunt we'd need. Do you?" Ives raised his eyebrows; the light from the coach side lamp flickered over his face, giving him a somewhat devilish look. Which was ridiculous.

"I could get it…" Den half turned away, tacitly acknowledging the truth of Ives' words.

"An engagement is *not* good enough," Katie said firmly. She *could not* go back and face her mother after being compromised. She just couldn't. The *fuss*! She looked up in appeal to Ives, who put a comforting arm around her shoulder and hugged her.

"All right, Kitty-kat, we'll get a special licence and be married in the morning."

"You can afford a special licence but you can't afford a trip to Gretna Green? They're hundreds of pounds!"

"Not for me!" Ives said. "We'll go to Truro. The bishop's my uncle, and my godfather. Mama's brother, you know." Of course they knew. Bishop Martin was a frequent visitor to Trengrouse Hall. "He'll hand over a licence. Sure to."

Hope rose in her. Mama wouldn't be happy about this marriage. A younger son wasn't what she'd had in mind at all. But it was a good deal better than being ruined.

And by now...Katie shuddered at the thought, but she knew her Mama would be demanding answers from all and sundry by now. Even if all she wanted to know was where the coach was, it would be damning.

"Yes," she said. "Let's go to Truro."

TRURO WAS a full seven miles away. The moon was down, but Gus rode ahead slowly on the bay mare and Ives took the reins, leaving Den and Katie to talk in the carriage.

"Are you sure this is what you want?" Denzell asked her quietly. "If you were engaged, perhaps you could let the gossip die away and then cry off in a few months."

"You know it *wouldn't* die away if I did that. Everyone would dig up every sordid detail–including those they made up! And Mama...can you *imagine*!"

Den shifted in his seat in agreement. "He's not the husband I would have chosen for you, Kitten."

"He's your best friend."

"Exactly! I know him. He's a good soul underneath but he's not the steadiest of companions. Harum scarum and a rapscallion. A stalwart friend, but not the man you want your sister to wed. Look at this bumble bath he's pulled you into!"

There was nothing in that she didn't know already. They'd all grown up together, after all; Petroc and Denzell best friends, with Ives tagging along behind the older boys, she and Kerenza bosom bows. Stories of Ives' smuggling escapades had made them all laugh…she didn't want a rapscallion for a husband, but the rules were strict, and no one knew that better than her mother's daughter. She'd have to make the best of it. It wasn't like Ives was a drunkard or a rake. She racked her brains for something positive to say.

"At least I won't have to travel a long way away from everything and everyone I know, which I might have done if I'd met someone in London next Season." That thought did cause her a pang. Not to have a debut Season! She had been looking forward to it for *so* long…

Tears filled her eyes, but she blinked them away. She couldn't let Den see.

She'd been on a course towards marriage her whole life, it seemed like. Every second sentence out of Mama's mouth nowadays was about her Season and 'prospects'.

Ives wasn't a good "prospect" but at least he was a *Trengrouse*. That counted for a lot in Cornwall, and perhaps Mama would be satisfied, although the way she went on about the Kelynacks coming over with the Conqueror, sometimes it felt like she'd only accept a Royal prince as a son-in-law. She *definitely* had her heart set on a title. Katie being plain "Mrs" wouldn't at all suit her.

It wasn't like Ives was penniless. The Trengrouses were all deep in the pocket.

A good family, a reasonable bridal Settlement, and, and—no, there were no other good aspects to this. Except that at least she didn't have to *flirt* with Ives.

Which made her wonder about the wedding night.

It was past midnight. *Tonight* would be her wedding night. She blushed in the darkness of the carriage. She wasn't entirely sure what was supposed to happen to a bride; Mama had always been very tight-lipped about it. But surely it wouldn't be *too* bad? Ives wouldn't *hurt* her. She could be sure of that, at least.

It was cold comfort. Her hands were shaking, so she clasped them together. She'd always hoped that she could find someone to love. Novel-reading nonsense, her mother had said. But people *did*! Surely they did. And then the wedding night might not be so bad?

She wished she knew more. How she wished it!

IVES FOLLOWED Gus's hand signals to avoid the worst of the potholes and ruts, and wished he had something else to take his mind off the present.

Married!

The uproar that would inevitably follow when they turned up tomorrow—no, today!—was exactly the kind of fuss he'd tried to avoid his whole life. Den's mother…he shuddered. It wasn't that she was a bad person. She just had Opinions, and was free with them. He'd have to turn her up sweet somehow, or Den's life wouldn't be worth living. Kitty-kat would be fine; she'd just move to Trengrouse Hall. She could have Demelza's old room next to his.

His thoughts stuttered on the idea of Kitty-kat and a bedroom. He couldn't…no, he just *couldn't*. Not Kitty-kat. She was like a sister to him. Besides, she probably wasn't ready for all that. She was only a babe.

They could put that off. Sufficient unto the day. One day, they'd want children. That was time enough to, to… well, to do the deed.

Oddly, that decision calmed him. If the whole thing turned out to be an absolute disaster, they could get an annulment.

CHAPTER 3

They arrived in Truro at dawn, and spent a little time at an inn, making themselves presentable and having something to eat.

"Can't land in the old's boy's lap before breakfast!" Ives said cheerfully, cutting slices of the ham the inn keeper had brought out. "Here you are, Kitty-kat."

Maybe when they were married she could get him to stop calling her that.

Her own parents had called each other "Kelynack" and "my lady" their whole lives until her father's death three years ago, but Ives wouldn't expect *that*, thank goodness!

Sitting in the inn parlour while Ives paid the shot was nerve-wracking, so when he came in a full half hour later, she glared at him. He grinned at her and held up a jeweller's box.

"I had to knock up the goldsmith. Can't get married without a ring!"

Oh. She hadn't even thought of that.

Getting into the Bishop's palace at Truro was remarkably easy—for a Trengrouse. Katie was astonished at the confidence with which Ives demanded an audience. The household staff all knew him, clearly, and were just as foolishly fond of him as the staff at home.

"His Grace will see you immediately, Mr Ives," the butler said.

Bishop Martin's study was a perfect bishop's room—filled with books, the light filtering through Gothic windows onto leather chairs and a paper-laden desk. He himself, though, looked more like an elderly lawyer's clerk, sharp-nosed and shrewd-eyed. But he smiled kindly at her.

It felt so *odd*. She'd known Bishop Martin all her life. How could she be here in front of him, asking for a *marriage* license?

Ives gave a concise and clear description of the fix they were in, and the bishop shook his head.

"Ives…"

Ives flung up a hand in the fencer's salute. "I know, I know, sir. You don't need to tell me. But now we have to repair the damage I've done. We are hoping you can issue a special licence for us, and then marry us."

"For free, no doubt?" Bishop Martin's voice was dry.

Ives grinned. "Call it a wedding present."

"If it weren't for this young lady, I'd tell you to go home and face the music, sir. But since it's Katherine Kelynack…" He patted her shoulder comfortingly. "You did very right to come here at once."

. . .

MORE QUICKLY THAN she would have believed, she was standing in front of the cathedral altar, hand in hand with Ives. They said their vows, and then he slid the ring onto her finger; it was warm from his hand, and fitted snugly, and felt oddly heavy.

"With this ring I thee wed, with my body I thee worship, with all my worldly goods I thee endow…" he said, his voice surprisingly calm. "In the name of the Father, and of the Son, and of the Holy Ghost."

Her own voice wavered a little as she joined in the "Amen".

The bishop told them they were man and wife.

Just like that.

They signed the register. The last time she'd ever sign that name. Now she was Katherine Trengrouse. A quiver went through her belly at the thought. It made her feel a little better that Ives' hand shook as he signed his name, too.

It was done.

She was married. She tucked her marriage lines away in her reticule. A talisman. The only thing which could protect her from ruin.

She would *not* burst into tears.

THEY STOOD OUTSIDE THE CATHEDRAL. Was Kitty-kat as unsure as he was about what to do next? She looked pale despite the warm morning sun.

"Best to head straight back. The horses should be rested by now. I'll ride back on your gelding, Ives, and break the news to everyone at the Hall." That was typical of Den. Kind as ever.

"Good man. That'll take the heat off Kitty-kat."

"We have to stop at home on the way, Ives," she said. "We have to tell Mama ourselves. She'd never forgive me otherwise."

Dammit, Den had got himself out of the hard job.

"That's true," Den agreed. "But I'll leave you to that one!? Ives punched him on the shoulder, but he just grinned and kissed Kitten's cheek. "It *will* be all right, my dear."

Blinking back tears, she nodded. Poor little lamb. If *he* felt all at sea, it must be worse for her. He was reaping what he'd sowed, but she'd done nothing.

Den ran off to the stables, and Ives offered her his arm.

"Seems deuced odd that we're married, doesn't it, chick?"

"*So* odd."

That made him feel better. They were in this together.

"MARRIED? *MARRIED?*" Lady Kelynack stared at them as though they were speaking Chinese.

"It was for the best, Lady Kelynack." Ives made his voice as calm as he could. Soothing, that was the ticket.

It didn't work.

"*MARRIED?*" Couldn't the woman find anything else to say?

Kitty-kat took her mother's elbow and led her to a chair, pushing her down firmly.

"It was the best solution, Mama. I would have been *ruined*."

Lady Kelynack blinked. Blinked again. The colour was coming back into her cheeks.

Kitty explained what had happened, her voice calm and even. By Jove, she was a trooper! No sign of tears or nerves. She'd always had heart.

"So it's *your* fault!" His – Good Lord, his Mama-in-law!- turned her eyes onto him accusingly. He spread his hands and nodded.–

"Yes. It's not Katherine's fault at all, Lady Kelynack. But Den and I thought–"

"Den! You and Den! What right had you to decide my daughter's fate?"

Oh, lud. "Den is my legal guardian, Mama," Kitty-kat said. Her back was straight as she sat on a sofa, and her blue eyes were surprisingly stern. "He had every right. And we were married in the cathedral, by Bishop Martin. Everything was quite respectable."

"Respectable!" The mention of the bishop soothed her a little, but not for long. "I had such *hopes!*" she wailed. "You might have had the Earl of Westholm!" Then the tears came, and a long monologue about the coming Season and how wonderful it would have been.

Belatedly, he realised that Kitty was beginning to tear up, too. Damn! He should have realised that losing a Season would be a bad thing to her, rather than the reprieve he'd have felt himself. Sighing, he resigned himself to squiring Kitty-kat around town for a few months. It was the least he could do.

"We can still go to London, Mama-in-law," he said. "We can stay at the townhouse in Grosvenor Square."

She blinked. Looked at him again, as if realising who he was. Not just scapegrace Ives, her son's best friend, but a Trengrouse.

"Settlements," she said firmly.

"Well, naturally! I'll discuss that with Den and your family lawyer."

The tears welled over again. "It's not what I wanted for you, Katherine," she hiccupped.

"I know, Mama." Kitty took her hand and let out a long breath. "But it's what happened."

The deadness in her voice was a cut to the bone. He wasn't *that* bad a catch, surely?

Well. If that's how it was, that's how it was. He was a disappointment to both of them. So be it.

Lady Kelynack insisted they stay for tea, and he was glad of it. By the end, his new mother-in-law had settled somewhat. At least she wasn't crying anymore.

"Time to go home," he said. They both looked up, startled, and then Kitty's face changed, becoming calm with that well bred blankness every young lady learned.

"Yes, of course. Mama, will you have Susan pack my things up and bring them to the Hall?"

"You wouldn't consider living here?"

Lady Kelynack stood and placed a hand on his sleeve. Behind her back, Kitty shook her head firmly. Thank God. There were limits.

"I'm afraid not. Trengrouse brides all go to the Hall."

Nodding, Lady Kelynack stood back and smoothed her dress down. "Tell your Mama I'll be over later today to- to discuss what we must do to damp down the scandal. We will put it around that it's a love match and that you eloped because I didn't approve of you, Ives. People will believe that."

Would they, b'god?

But, shamingly, he knew they would.

Anger surged in him; he didn't know exactly who he was angry with, but he'd like to plant *someone* a facer.

"Let's go, Kitty-kat."

Time to go home and face the music.

CHAPTER 4

*B*y the time they reached Trengrouse Hall, it was after noon. The Hall lay somnolent in the summer sunshine. The front door was ajar, as it often was on fine days on his father's orders, to let in the sea air.

He and Kitty-kat walked into the hall to find his brother Petroc embracing Lady Beatrice Marlowe.

"Tally-ho and away!" Ives said. He couldn't help it. For days, he'd been watching Petroc's silent yearning after Beatrice, and her yearning after him, with equally silent amusement.

Petroc and Beatrice broke apart, faces flaming.

"We're betrothed!" Petroc said hurriedly.

"I can top that, brother. We're married!"

"*Ives!*" Kitty hissed at him and the other two surged forward with surprised congratulations. "We're supposed to see your parents first!"

Damn. But how could he resist the opportunity to cap Petroc? It was irresistible. Besides, Den must have been here hours ago.

The noise brought the rest of the family out, without Den, and it became clear that he had never arrived, nor sent word of what had happened.

So they had the chance to pull off the true-love elopement story. The family hubbubbed around, full of questions and a rather strange hilarity.

"Typical Ives" seemed to be the general consensus, which was a huge exaggeration. Lion grinned at him and made drinking gestures to imply he'd been drunk. He scowled at him. As if he'd subject Kitty-kat to that.

"But, but *why?*" his mother asked, hugging Kitty.

"My Mama–"

Ives cut in to spare her the lie.

"Kitty's Mama doesn't approve of me as her husband. Too harum scarum and no title." Come to think of it, that *wasn't* a lie. He felt more cheerful, and tucked Kitten's hand under his arm. "So we ran away to Truro and m'godfather married us by special licence!"

"That was very silly of her," Melissa said calmly. "You will make an excellent husband, Twin."

He smiled gratefully at her.

The earl approached with a brow of thunder. Ives swallowed nervousness down.

"Lady Kelynack is right. This was a scandalous way to treat poor Katherine." He turned to Kitten with a beaming smile. "But I will say, you have *excellent* taste! Welcome to the family, Katie!" He flung out an arm to Beatrice. "And to you, my dear! This is a fine day for the Trengrouses, to welcome two wonderful young women to the fold."

And that took the attention off them. Petroc's betrothal was immediately the main topic as they all swept into the big drawing room for afternoon tea. It stung a little. Understandable—since Petroc had almost died losing a leg at Waterloo, the women of the family had been hovering over him like hens with one chick. And Beatrice was almost as well known to them all as Kitty-kat was, since Beatrice's mother and his were bosom-bows.

Besides, their own marriage was done. A settled thing. While Petroc's gave the girls (except Melissa, who'd gone off to read in the library) the chance to plan a splendid bridal.

He sat next to his *wife* (how strange that was) and watched her face. This was what his stupidity had cost her: all the planning and excitement and happiness of an engagement. He'd have to make it up to her somehow.

That London Season, perhaps, even though he'd hate it.

. . .

Melissa appeared in the doorway, and tipped her head in their old signal that she needed him. He excused himself and went out to the hall.

"I have to go to London," she said. Urgent, which wasn't like her. "Charles has been lured into something dangerous. I have to go and decode a message on the way."

His gut lurched. Charles Goddard, Earl of Westholm, was Melissa's best friend. And maybe more. On any other day, he'd have been rousting up the stableboy and getting the carriage out for her.

Today…he cast a glance back at the drawingroom. Kitty. He couldn't—he just *couldn't* —abandon her.

"I can't go with you, Twin. Any other time…but it would be wrong to desert Katie today."

A flash of annoyance gave way to pity in her face, and he felt that like a dagger strike.

If Melissa was sorry for him, he must look upset. He had to find a solution for her.

"Lion is leaving this morning," he said. "He's giving Felix a lift back to London."

"Perfect." Melissa's maid arrived with her valise and what seemed like a worried face. "Take that out to the stable," Melissa told her, "and get it put on Mr Endellion's coach."

"Yes, miss."

As if called, Lion came down the stairs carrying his greatcoat, and readily agreed to take her.

Then there was a whole hullabaloo from his parents about Melissa going off unchaperoned—as if two brothers weren't enough respectability! But it was all sorted out and the three of them went off on some kind of adventure.

It hurt to see them go without him. He should have been the one to protect his twin. *He* should have been the one to help her.

But, unlike Lion and Felix, he was now a married man, and had responsibilities. It felt like sacks full of lead had been tied to him. He wasn't sure he could stand it.

Katie sat quietly while the Trengrouses fought in the hall about Melissa going to London. None of her business. It was sorted out and they all came back and settled in as though nothing had happened. Unlike Mama, the Trengrouses never held grudges. Once a fight was over, it was done.

So the Trengrouse women and Beatrice Marlowe sat down and blithely talked about weddings while Ives and the earl listened with amazing patience.

She would have liked to plan her own wedding. Blinking back tears, she felt Ives watching her. He'd been splendid, really. No second of hesitation in saving her reputation, though she knew him well enough to know he'd no wish to marry *anyone*. Especially not someone he wasn't in love with.

There had been that Scottish girl—Janet? Jeanette?—he'd been head over ears about when he was seventeen. And then there'd been Charity, the vicar's daughter at Swain Cove, who hadn't even cast a glance his way. Both of them had been a few years older than he was. And now he was stuck with a girl not even nineteen yet, years before he'd meant to marry.

Her body was full of swirling emotions, but the strongest was anger. It wasn't *right* that their lives should be pushed into this course, just because of some ridiculous rules for debutantes! It wasn't *fair*! Time to get out of here before she burst into tears and shattered the illusion of a happy elopement.

She took in a deep breath, and rose. Immediately, the chattering stopped and every eye was on her.

"I'm sorry, I'm a little tired." She spoke directly to the countess. Oh, Lord, what should she call her? She'd always called her Aunt Maria! Should she call her Mama-in-law?

The countess also rose, smiling.

"Of course you are. We're full to the

rafters at the moment, so I'm afraid you'll have to share Ives' room tonight."

Ives' room. A blush swept up over her face and knowing smiles were turned away from her. Such consideration, but equally embarrassing.

She followed Aunt Maria out of the room and up the staircase to Ives' room—the smallest of the family bedchambers, but valued by him because of the giant oak outside the window, which allowed him to come and go whenever he pleased.

Lud. She knew so much about him, and yet, as a husband, she knew nothing. Including when he'd want...marital relations. This *was* their wedding night.

As they came in, Aunt Maria gestured to her to sit on one of the armchairs by the fire, while she took the other.

"I'm glad to have this time with you, my dear. Of course, I'm delighted that you've joined the family, but why did you not come to me? I could have reasoned with your Mama."

Oh, how she *hated* this lying!

"I…it was a, a, a spur of the moment thing."

"I see. So the megrim last night? That was a ploy?"

"Oh, no! I was quite ill. But, well, Ives went with me to drive me home, to, to make sure I was all right, and then Den came and said everyone knew and we just thought— we just thought it would be *easier* to get married."

The countess' eyes were kind and far too understanding.

"I see. One of Ives' starts, was it? Are you sure you weren't pushed into it, Katie, because of the gossip? It's not too late for an annulment is it?"

So there *had* been gossip! It helped to know that.

"Oh no! But…but I'm sure. Den wanted us to simply get engaged, but Mama…I was the one who said marriage would be best."

Aunt Maria smoothed down her skirts and stood. "Well then, the family will stand behind you." She stared into the distance for a moment. "This may be the making of Ives. And we couldn't be happier than to have you as a daughter-in-law."

Impulsively, Katie jumped up and hugged her. "Thank you so much, Aunt Maria—oh! should I call you Mama-in-law?"

"Oh no, my dear! Why break a lifelong habit! I'm quite happy with Aunt. Once I'm a grandmother, we can think about changing my name."

She went out, closing the door quietly behind her. Grandmother.

That meant children. Best not to think about that right now.

Katie looked around the room. So masculine. So Ives. Fishing flies pinned to the four-poster's curtains. A rod in the corner. The smell of brandy and cologne. On the chest of drawers, a scatter of shirt studs and a discarded riding crop. On the washstand, his shaving gear.

She didn't belong here. Thank God she'd have her own room once all the visitors left.

They kept country hours at the Hall when there wasn't a party, so dinner would be soon. She didn't even have her own clothes. And where was Den?

Hot helplessness surged up in her chest. This was her life now. All alone in someone else's family.

Sitting down in the chair, she burst into tears.

CHAPTER 5

Her mother found her there—fortunately, after she'd stopped crying. But the marks of tears were plain on her face.

"Well may you cry!" Mama said. "If you'd only been strong enough to stay at the ball- Megrims! A lady never gives in to illness! If you'd *stayed-*"

"But I didn't," Katie whispered. She could feel the tears climbing again, but childhood necessity had built a habit of not crying in front of her mother, and it helped her now. "I didn't, Mama, and now I'm married, and we have to make the best of it."

Mama let out a long, exasperated sigh, but let it go. She sat on the bed—a thing Katie had been scolded for over and over. She'd *never* seen her mother do it. It was a measure of how unsettled Mama was, and that brought a tight, hard ball of guilt into Katie's chest.

"Well. Yes. Tonight is your wedding night." Mama's face was red. Was she *blushing*? "I suppose I should warn you…"

Katie was torn; she wanted so desperately to know what to expect, but she'd rather *anyone* else to be her informant. Aunt Maria, for example.

"There's only one thing you really need to know," her mother said. "You must *never* appear forward to your husband. You must wait until he makes the first move. Only strumpets show, er…desire. Only women of low character initiate…anything. A man wants that from his mistress, not from his wife. From his wife, he wants decorum." She sniffed. "And acceptance, of course. You must not turn away his advances, but you must *never* encourage him, or he will think you quite beyond the pale." She nodded with certainty, as if her job was done, and rose. "Wash your face before you come downstairs."

Mama hurried out as though she feared any questions. She paused by the door, her back to her daughter. "Trust your husband to guide you," she said, then swept out and closed the door with a thunk behind her.

Katie sat still for a long moment. Trust your husband. But trust him to do *what?*

DINNER, and port in the library, when all the talk was about Petroc and Beatrice's plans to start a horse stud.

Only Percival Muffet sat by him and mentioned his marriage.

"Elopement sounds like a topping idea," he said wistfully.

Ives had watched Muffet and Kerenza

dance around each other over the past few days, and he laughed shortly.

"If Papa gives his blessing to the match, you'll never get Keri to agree to that! She'll want the whole dollop—all in lace at St George's, Hanover Square, with all her sisters and sisters-in-law to stand up with her!"

Muffet gazed at him with an odd smile. "So I should hope he *doesn't* give his blessing, and take you as my model?"

"Oh, no, my old trout! Never take *me* as a model if you want my family to approve of you."

There was just too much truth in that, and he could hear his own bitterness. He jumped up, avoiding Muffet's eyes.

He was nothing to this family. His marriage was nothing. He was just a young fool whose actions meant nothing. Well, if that was what they wanted, that's what they would get.

Ives poured himself a double brandy and went to join the discussion of Blackfoot's new foal.

· · ·

With a practised eye, Ives considered how much he was staggering up the stairs and judged he'd had two too many.

Positively restrained of him under the circumstances.

His father and brothers and the other male guests still present after the ball had joked with him about his elopement but the subject had soon dropped in favour of the current price of tin and the prospects of trade with France now Bonaparte had been defeated.

None of which he'd been interested in. If it had been the price of corn, now… he could have held his own on that.

Hesitating outside his bedroom door, he was beset by doubt. Did one knock at one's own door if one's *wife* was inside?

He blushed that he might catch her *en deshabille*, and knocked.

"C-come in."

Was that small voice Kitty-kat? He pushed open the door and peered around.

There she was, sitting up in bed, the covers pulled right up, her shining blonde hair spilling over her shoulders. She'd always been a dashed pretty girl.

Her face was pale. Poor Kit. Probably worrying he'd demand his rights. As if he would.

He wandered in and waved his hand. "Doan' worry, Kitty-kat. Wouldn't think of it."

His valet had made himself scarce, damn him. How was a man to get his boots off?

Sitting on the chair by his desk, he tried his best but his Hesssians were stuck tight. He gave one a good yank and fell off the chair, lying there for a while, staring at the coffered ceiling. Jolly clever how they'd put those corners together.

"Oh, for Heaven's sake!" A tug on his left foot made him look—Kitty-kat was pulling off his other boot. She looked at him sternly. "You're foxed."

"Devil a bit!" he said. "Just a little top-lofty. Barely cut at all."

"Mmm-hmmm." She managed to get the boot off and set both of them outside the door, ready for the boot boy. His valet wouldn't like that, but serve him right if they came back with a thumbprint on them.

"Come *on*, Ives. Get up and get into bed."

He could do that. Of course he could. And he did…slowly.

Sleeping in his shirt seemed like the best policy. It was almost as long as a nightgown, anyway.

He fumbled his way under the sheets, and turned to Kitty, who was back with the covers pulled up to her chin. That scared look had come back. He patted her hand with clumsy sincerity.

"S'all right, pet. We can wait. Until we want bub-bub…babies."

That would do it. *Good man,* he thought. *Well done.* He went to sleep immediately, feeling virtuous and very grown-up.

•　•　•

WELL. *Well.*

Katie didn't know whether to be relieved or insulted. Was she so unattractive? Part of her was desolate at the thought. To be married to a man who didn't desire one…

Ives was curled up like a hedgehog, his black curls falling over his eyes. Her anger melted away. Silly guffin. And so kind, to reassure her and give her the time she needed.

Relief won.

CHAPTER 6

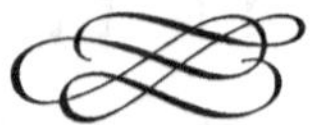

Kitty was gone when he woke up. The sun was high, too. He rang the bell, holding his head, which ached damnably. Served him right.

Neale, his valet, arrived with a tankard of small ale which Ives drank with gratitude while Neale collected hot water from the footman waiting outside the door.

Shaving made his head spin a little, but the ale was helping keep the nausea down.

'Kit- Mrs Trengrouse?' he asked. At least Kitty was the only Mrs Trengrouse. His mother was the Countess, Lady Trengrouse, and Ellestryn was Lady Penoch, since Locryn, her husband, was Viscount Penoch. Melza was Mrs Mandeville. She was widowed, though, so she might have a different name someday.

"With the ladies in the morning room, sir." Neale was stiff with disapproval.

"Don't be so Friday-faced, man!"

"Will madam be moving to her own room today, sir?"

"Is that what's got you so out of sorts?"

Neale sniffed. "I *had* thought, sir, that it would be my privilege to dress you for your wedding."

Oh, Lord. He felt slighted.

"Well, you did. You dressed me for the ball, which was the same thing."

"You married in your *ball clothes*, sir?"

"Perfectly respectable."

The poor man looked genuinely upset. And Neale was such a right one! They'd been in many a scrape together where he'd come out trumps. Ives put a hand on his shoulder.

"We couldn't let *anyone* know, Neale. Even Sir Denzell only found out by chance."

Neale's long face relaxed, knowing how close Ives and Den were. Odd, really, since Den was Petroc's age, but after Petroc joined the Army and Demelza was married, Den had been at a bit of a loose end, and since they both loved to sail, they'd fallen into company.

"I hope you'll accept my best wishes for a very happy marriage, Mr Ives."

"Thank you."

"Very good, sir. Mr Walton is expecting you in half an hour."

Excellent. Just enough time to break his fast and look in on Kitty-kat.

He dressed with speed and headed for the morning room. Neale would see to it that Cook sent some victuals in to him. Great thing, having a solid valet.

Sure enough, he'd no more than sat down at the morning room table where the ladies were having tea than a tray arrived via footman with bread and cheese and apples and more ale.

"Ah, that's the stuff."

"Been overdoing it?" Demelza asked drily. She looked rather well this morning, but Kitten seemed tired. No wonder.

"No more than I should, dear sister." He smiled at Kitty-kat and she managed a smile back. She twisted her wedding ring on her finger. Must feel odd. He had a ring of his grandfather's but he'd never liked the feel of it. "Moving into your own room today, lamb?"

"Trying to get rid of her already?" Ellestryn put in. Her smile was wry; she was joking.

"She can stay forever as far as I'm concerned, but Neale is fretting that she'll take all the cupboard space!"

That made everyone laugh, and Kitty relaxed. His mother put a hand on her arm. "Well..." The tone made them all stop and stare at her. She spoke to Demelza. "I hope you don't mind, Mellie, but I rather thought we'd give Katherine your room once you're gone."

"Oh." An odd look came across Demelza's face. "That *would* be the most suitable one, but, em…I was planning to stay a little longer, Mama."

"Lovely! Well then… Petroc's room, since he will be at Semper House from now on— that is the plan, isn't it, Beatrice?"

Lady Beatrice nodded. "The sea bathing is so good for his leg." Petroc had lost the lower part of his leg at Waterloo and had been staying with Beatrice's mother in Swain Cove to rehabilitate by sea-bathing each day. Lord, they had a big family! Kitty was following the conversation without a moment's confusion. Thank God he didn't have to explain it all to her.

"Petroc's room, then."

As if that were a signal, all the women stood up and headed for the door. He scrambled to his feet and managed to catch Kitty's arm as she went past. She paused, looking up at him.

Jove she was pretty! He'd never really paid much attention to her before. At least he'd have a lovely face looking at him over breakfast every morning.

"All right, Kitty-kat?" he asked.

She nodded, smiling, but pulled away to follow the others, saying, "Don't call me that!" over her shoulder.

All right then.

Now to the estate office. Walton was his father's steward and, theoretically, was training him to take over the stewardship one day.

Walton had showed no enthusiasm for the task. Hard to blame a man for not wanting to train himself out of a job, but the fellow was sixty if he were a day, and surely ought to be looking to retirement.

Today they were going over the double entry bookkeeping system. He was going to have the devil of a job to pretend he didn't know it, given that he'd been helping Grandma Smith keep the smuggler's books in Swain Cove since he was fourteen.

She'd been a good teacher, too.

There was a book about it in the library. Written by some Italian. He could pretend he'd read that.

By the time he left to join the party for dinner, the best part of the day already gone, he'd put an extra furrow in Walton's brow through his apparently miraculous devotion to studying accounting.

He'd like to tell the man that he didn't want his job, but the truth was…no, the truth was he *didn't* want that job, but only because Walton worked for his father. As steward, he'd be forever the youngest son, tied to his family's apron strings.

Even the reaction to his sudden marriage – "Oh, it's only Ives!" Lion had said. As if that made it a play marriage, not real and not serious.

There'd been just enough truth in that to hurt.

CHAPTER 7

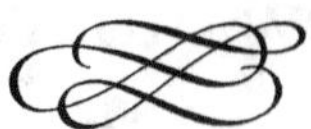

For Katie, the end-of-summer days passed with an odd sense of *déja vu*. So many of her past summers had been spent at Trengrouse Hall: picnics and sailing days and riding in the cool mornings, and helping bring in and preserve all the bounty of the walled gardens.

This summer, the only difference was that she didn't go home at dusk.

Instead, she wandered up to her own room, which still smelt slightly of gun oil and boot polish, where her maid Susan was waiting, as if she'd never lived anywhere else.

It was odd. It was *deuced* odd, as Ives would say. The days seemed to pass her like water, not quite substantial; nothing you could get a grip on.

There were a few differences.

She visited her mother once a week, on Fridays, since Mama's 'at home' days were Tuesday and Thursdays, and this let her escape the inquisitorial gossips. Mama, at first desolated by her marriage, had decided that having her so close was a blessing and was already dropping heavy hints about grandchildren.

The oddest thing was that she had no duties.

At home, she was being trained to run a household, so Mama had delegated a number of routine tasks to her: approving the menu, or deciding which linens could be darned and which should be turned into cleaning rags. She had her own accounts to do, and her mother's as well, and a score of other things.

At Trengrouse Hall, every task already

belonged to someone else. No one needed her for anything more than her company.

Well, it had always been like that, of course—one didn't set even a regular guest to work. But now she wasn't a guest.

She approached the countess.

"My dear, of course we can find something for you to do!" Which wasn't exactly what she'd asked. "I'll get Kerenza on to that. I'm sure she'll be glad to share her own duties with you."

Kerenza, though, shrugged it off. "Don't ask me. Melza's sailed in and taken everything over that I usually do. Let's just amuse ourselves!"

Keri was full of plans to go up to London for the Season, and assumed that Katie would come with her.

"We'll shop ourselves silly!" she proclaimed joyfully. Katie smiled and nodded, but she wasn't at all sure that Ives intended for them to go.

That night, she knocked on his door. When he opened it, he seemed surprised and perhaps a bit nervous to see her. Did he think she was going to demand babies? Not very complimentary.

She sat stiffly in the chair by the dresser and regarded him. She'd barely seen him, except at dinner. The men and women of the house lived separate lives, for the most part, and he'd supposedly been busy with the estate manager, Mr Walton, although her maid confided that "Mr Ives" dipped out of those meetings as often as he went to them.

When they did meet, there was an odd formality between them. She didn't know how to get past that.

"Keri thinks I'm going to London with her in October." She watched his face intently; he winced, but immediately covered it up with a smile.

"Well, of course! I promised you a London Season, and you shall have one. You'll have more fun as a young matron than as a debutante, you know."

She hadn't considered that, but it was

true. A gurgle of laughter burst out of her. "I can chaperone Keri!"

"God help London!"

And suddenly they were back to being friends again, as they had been before they were married.

"I know you don't want to come…"

"Had to happen," he said philosophically. "Mama was planning to take me this year to squire Keri and Melissa around. At least this way I won't have all the matchmaking Mamas after me."

"Because you're such a catch!"

"M'dear, I'm a prize of the first water!" He paraded around the room, his thumbs in his lapels, in a caricature of a vain dandy. He could always make her laugh.

"Seriously, Ives…" Now she was shy. They'd never discussed money. She had no idea of her husband's financial position. No idea where she should go for her own pin money. She was down to her last guinea. "I will have to do some shopping…"

"Of course, Kitty-kat. Just have them send the bills to me at Trengrouse House."

"But…do I have a set allowance? How much…" she trailed off. It was so *vulgar*, having to talk about money.

"Oh." He was discomfitted too. "Oh. Yes. Of course you have an allowance. I went over all that with Den. It's paid into your account quarterly."

"My account?"

"You have an account on the estate, just as I have. Walton will tell you how much is in it at any time. If you need funds, he'll advance them to you. In London, it will be Solomon, m'father's man of business."

Ask Mr Walton? He had always disapproved of them, looking down his nose at their childish antics, even when they had *been* children.

"I don't think…"

"Walton's not that scary, m'dear. I'll get an advance from him each quarter and keep it for you, if you prefer."

"Oh, *thank* you, Ives! Yes, I would prefer

that." He was smiling down at her with avuncular kindness; that didn't feel right. He was barely older than she was. "Do *you* have to ask Walton?"

"Lord, no! I have my own banking. I have an account on the estate, of course, but I barely use it."

"So…you have your own funds?"

"Did you think you'd married a poor relation? Don't worry, Kitty-kat, I'm a warm man!"

He laughed at her but it felt wrong that she didn't know just how they stood. Men treated women like children.

"Don't call me that! My name is Katie. And it would serve you right if I bankrupted you with modiste's bills!"

That just made him laugh harder. "You'd have to buy a good few dresses to do that, Kitten. Silk and velvet and studded with diamonds!"

She threw a cushion at him, but ended up laughing in the end.

· · ·

THERE WAS SO MUCH about this marriage business that he hadn't expected! He'd thought Den would have told Katie about her allowance and how to access it, but evidently he'd believed that was Ives' own job. Perhaps he was right.

He'd set something up with Walton to give Kit her pin money every quarter; and make it generous, too. No need for Kitten to go without; it wasn't as though he was dependent on his father, although he wasn't sure she had really understood that.

All the Trengrouse boys had been given shares in the mines and other business interests on their 15th birthdays. Petroc had given Keri some of his shares for her 18th, and the men of the family had decided that was a good idea. Melza didn't need anything. She had a generous widow's portion, and if the babe she was carrying was a boy, she'd be living at Mandeville's estate in Gloucestershire for life. If a girl, she'd move to the Dower House. She was set.

But Melissa should also have something

to fall back on, so he and the others had put together a parcel of shares for her, too.

The Settlement he'd made on Katie gave her financial security if he died, but her allowance came straight from his coffers, and that meant she was dependent on him. Being a dependant was a deucedly uncomfortable situation. Perhaps he should make the Settlement over to her absolutely, rather than it going to her after his death?

But what would she *do* with it?

He lay in bed with his hands behind his head, staring at the canopy. It wasn't as though he was going to hold the purse strings too tight.

Pshaw! It was all too complicated for this time of night. As long as he made funds available to her, it would be fine.

"Tenants' Day tomorrow!" the countess said. "Help me look over the visitor's china, Katherine?"

Something to do! Finally! Katie eagerly

followed the countess into the china room, with three maids trailing behind. The "visitor's china" was in the lowest cupboard; this wasn't one of the Sèvres patterns. A nice willow pattern in English stoneware—a little old-fashioned, but still pretty.

"Take it to the morning room and check that none of it is chipped, if you please, my dear."

The maids followed her, arms full of plates and bowls. The smallest tweeny was struggling, so Katie took a pile of dinner plates from her.

The morning room table had a calico tablecloth on it, protecting it for the inspection. There was so much to learn about running a household! Mama had taught her a great deal, but things like calico tablecloths and visitor's china were another world. At least she was *part* of it this time, doing something useful.

Elestryn was waiting at the table.

Oh. No doubt she'd take over. It was her

place to do so, of course, as the wife of the eldest son…

Katie came around the table, keeping her face in a smile. It wasn't Elestryn's fault. There was simply no real place for the wife of the youngest boy, even in a house as big as Trengrouse Hall. All she could do was *help*.

As she reached the table, Ives came in through the door to the hall. He smiled at her. "Kitty-kat! I have some news."

She set the pile of plates down so hard that the top one broke, but she didn't care. Devil take him!

"My *name* is Katherine. You can use that, or Katie. But I've told you before, *never* call me Kitty, and especially not *Kitty-kat!*"

She ran out. The garden. She could find a place to hide there, and conceal the tears which scorched her face.

WHAT THE DEVIL? Ives stared after Kitty—*Katie*—dumbstruck. The maids avoided his eyes, fussing with the china on the table.

Elestryn gave a jerk of her head, and the three of them rushed out with relief.

"You've gone cack-handed about this whole marriage," Elestryn said, "and if you don't go after her, you won't *have* a wife."

That hit him below the heart, and he gasped.

"I mean it, Ives. She's been drooping around here like a wet hen, and you haven't even noticed. Don't pretend you're in love with her. She knows that. And when two people marry for reasons other than love, they'd better be good friends and have a common purpose, or it goes very badly."

Ives looked at her sharply. Was she talking about her own marriage to Locryn? It had been an arranged match...never mind that.

He nodded at Elestryn and went out the door Kitty—*Katie*—had used. Goddam it. He and Den had called her variations of Kitty-kat her whole life, and she'd never objected before.

Or had she? He had a vague recollection

of her saying something... Elestryn was right. He'd better start paying more attention.

The garden was quiet, and he could hear light running footsteps going towards the summerhouse. Give her time to get there and calm down a little.

Start with an apology. That was the way.

When he rounded a corner of the hedge and came to the summerhouse, Katie was sitting on one of the benches which went right around the outside, wiping her cheeks. She looked up as he approached, and her eyes widened. Was that *fear*? Surely his little Kitten couldn't be *afraid* of him?

"I'm sorry," he said immediately. "You're right. I shouldn't call you that."

She blinked up at him, astonished. So that was what she thought of him? That he'd try to blame *her*? Then tears welled up in her eyes again. He sat down next to her and took her hand.

"What's all this then?"

Katie turned her head away, but he took

her chin and turned it back. It hurt him—actually *hurt* him—to see her like this. "What is it, wife?"

She promptly burst into sobs. Baffled, he put his arm around her shoulder and let her weep against his chest. What could be upsetting her so? By God, if any of the others had been cruel to her, he'd take them down a peg or two! She was his wife and they'd better treat her as such! He kissed the top of her head. She had such a sweet nature, she wouldn't know how to deal with that.

"Has anyone been mean to you?" She shook her head against his shoulder.

"No, no," she gasped. Fool that he was, he *had* a kerchief! He pulled it out and gave it to her; as though that was a signal, she sat up and dried her eyes.

"Then what's the matter?"

"I don't *belong* here!" It came out as a cry. He winced.

"I know it might take a while to settle in–"

She straightened and glared at him. "It's

not a matter of settling in! I have nothing to *do*. They include me in tasks just to be kind! Being 'Ive's wife' doesn't give me any respon-sibility at all. I'm just…like the youngest daughter of the house."

That struck a nerve. He had no real role here either, with Walton delaying bringing him into the estate management. He hadn't stopped to think what that meant for Katie. Well. Perhaps his news might change things. He'd intended to go alone, but it might do Katie good to get away from the place.

"I can see that it might be hard," he said carefully. "Would you like to have a break?"

"It's too early to go to London." Her voice was flat and not at all like her. She was nor-mally so full of life. It cut to his heart.

"Not London. Norfolk. A place called Kirwich Manor, in Little Foxbury."

"Norfolk?"

Ives pulled the letter out of his pocket. "I have an estate there. Nothing like this–" He waved his hand at the Hall. "My godfather left it to me. You know, Mama's younger brother, Moxham. Moxham Martin." He grinned. What a name! Some family name that got passed down. Thank God his mother had refused to use it on any of them.

His uncle had been a frequent visitor to Trengrouse Hall. Katie was sure to remember him.

"Uncle Moxham?"

"That's the one. Since my uncle died, the place has been run by his steward, Reynolds, but the man is dying. I need to go and make sure he's being looked after and all is well. Would you like to come with me?"

The light returned to her eyes and the lilt to her voice.

"Oh, *yes!*"

Crisis averted. For now. It was tricky. He could see that there was little for her to do here. Normally, a marriage meant children, and then the wife had something to occupy her time, and a place that others recognised, and—well, a kind of status. His status in the family had always been pretty low (his own scapegrace fault), and the fact that they'd all known Katie since her birth probably meant that they treated her just as she said, like the youngest daughter. But a daughter was someone whose place in the world would come with her marriage. An elevation not available to Katie. She'd be stuck as the lowest rung on the ladder for good.

He tucked her hand in his arm as they strolled back along the neatly raked gravel. He'd have to give this a lot more thought.

CHAPTER 8

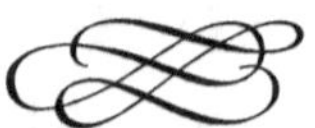

It was a long journey to Little Foxbury, the village nearest Kirwich Hall. Seven days on the road. So Ives had delayed their departure in order to send a messenger ahead to book their rooms; four of them, one each and one each for Susan and Neale, who travelled sitting backwards in their chaise. Even Ives wasn't harumscarum enough to travel without a valet. Katie was conscious, though, of Susan's gaze on them all through the journey. It made for oddly stilted conversation. At least none of them were prone to travel-sickness.

It was exciting, however, to leave Cornwall. The furthest she had been was Portsmouth. This was travelling through entirely different countrysides. Up through the downs and across the Chiltern Hills to Luton. A stop in Oxford where Ives walked her around his old college (imagine that he had taken a First in Mathematics – why had no one ever mentioned that at the Hall?).

"Do you miss it?"

He shouted with laughter. "Lord, no! The numbers were fine, but the life was too closed in and confined for me."

He went out that evening to swim at somewhere called Stump's Pool, and came back late, well after their normal dinner time. She peeped out of her room when she heard him come and he hailed her.

"Katie! Sorry I'm late. I met some old chums and was inveigled into having a drink."

His jacket was hooked over his shoulder, and the fine linen of his shirt clung to his chest, still damp. The light from his single candle laid a gold sheen on his cheekbones. Her heart sped up and she felt off kilter, as though he were a stranger. She hadn't realised he was so muscular; so *adult*. He was more handsome than she allowed herself to admit. A blush heated her cheeks.

He was looking at her strangely. She cleared her throat.

"That must have been nice for you."

"But I'm a beast to have kept you waiting. I'll only be a moment."

Sure enough, a moment later he was knocking on her door to take her down. She'd got control of herself by then. How foolish, to have the vapours over Ives! Still, all the way down the stairs she was conscious of the strength of his arm under her hand.

At dinner, Ives waited until the innkeeper had left the room

"There's something I have to tell you before we get to Kirwich." Ives looked oddly strained. What on Earth could it be?

"Yes?" Katie tried to make her voice encouraging.

"It's about Reynolds."

"The steward?"

"Yes. You should know that my uncle's will gave him the right to live at Kirwich Manor until his death, and the right to draw on the estate during that time."

"That's unusual. Your uncle must have thought highly of him." Very highly. She'd never heard of an employee being treated so.

"Mm. The thing is… he was rather more than a steward. He and Uncle Moxham…" Ives let his voice trail off meaningfully.

Was *that* all? As if she hadn't known Felix Trengrouse her whole life.

"They were like Felix?"

"Oh, I *wish* Felix could find someone like Reynolds! Uncle Moxham and he were like a happy old married couple." Ives seemed relieved. "I forgot you knew about Felix."

"How could you forget the way he positively *pined* after our undergroom for *months*.

You and Den teased him every chance you had!"

He flushed. "I didn't realise you'd heard all that. You were a tad young then to find out about such things."

Katie shrugged. "Better early than late. Otherwise you'd be in a pickle, trying to explain it all to me now!"

They met each other eyes and began to laugh helplessly.

"God's truth, I would be in a pickle!" he gasped. "Thank God you're so worldly-wise."

Katie leant back and smiled. Her husband was starting to realise she wasn't a little girl any more. A curl of some feeling twisted under her heart. Perhaps she should try to show him she was an adult in other ways?

She wished she knew how to.

"Mr Trengrouse gave you notice that we'd be arriving." Katie stared at the housekeeper sternly. "But this place is thick with dust!" The hall was beautifully furnished in the

French style, but every delicate piece needed a thorough clean.

"Only a day's notice, madam!" Mrs Barber protested. "I didn't have time to do more than your bedchambers. Mr Reynolds, he laid off the staff once the master went! Said it wasn't no use nevermind to keep the whole house up just for himself."

"Only a day?" The woman nodded earnestly. Really, Ives was a fool sometimes. "Well, we can't go on like this. Hire a few women from Little Foxbury to come up and give the whole place a thorough going over. What about a cook?"

"Oh, no, missus. The master had a proper chef. Liked his vittles, the master. But Mr Reynolds, he didn't feel right keeping him on."

"We'll need to hire a cook too, then. I suppose, until they arrive, I can manage."

"*You*, missus?"

"Certainly." Her mother was of the opinion that the lady of the house had to be able to do *anything* she asked of her staff—

except empty the chamber pots, of course. And the laundry, which was back-breaking work. A lady needed to know how things were done, so she could supervise and pick up on problems. So Katie had been taught to cook, and do plain sewing as well as fancy, and could dust and mop if she absolutely had to.

She hoped she wouldn't have to, but they couldn't live like this.

The tour continued. It was a lovely house. Not a huge hall, like Trengrouse, but perfect for a single family. On the ground floor were an office (Reynolds', no doubt, since it was scrupulously clean and tidy), a library leading on to the dining room, a morning room and other necessary spaces, like the kitchen, scullery, butler's pantry and a small offshoot of that which held china. No old willow pattern here—the master had preferred French products here, too, and the shelves were full of Sèvres. Upstairs was the main salon, a small withdrawing room she could use as her own, and three bedrooms.

On the next floor, half was servant's quarters and half–

"This is the old nursery and the school-room next door," Mrs Barber said, with an assessing look at Katie's waistline.

"Very good." She kept her voice level. "No doubt we'll have need of them *eventually.*" Perhaps. She drew in a breath, holding back silly tears. Sooner or later Ives would want an heir. She could wait for that.

The housekeeper was disappointed, clearly, but she led the way to the attics, which were full of the flotsam and jetsam of an old house.

"The first thing is to clear out the morning room and the small withdrawing-room," Katie said. "If we can get that done the rest can wait until tomorrow."

"Yes, missus."

She really ought to insist that Mrs Barber call her "ma'am" or "madam". But she rather liked the sound of "missus". It reminded her that she was here by right, as a married woman, not simply Ive's friend's little sister.

"Show me the kitchen." She rolled up her sleeves. "I'll get started on the dinner while you and Gladys can tackle the morning room."

IVES HELD the glass of laudanum to Reynolds' lips. The old man took a sip, sighed, and laid back against his pillows. His face was so pale Ives found it hard to believe he still had blood under his skin.

What to say? What *was* there to say?

"Don't worry about anything," he managed. "I'll take over the estate."

"And... your good wife will manage... the house." Just a rasping whisper, with gulps of air between words. "Your uncle would be so... glad. Sorry... he didn't meet her."

At least there was some good news he could share. "Oh, he met her! I've known Katie my whole life. Her brother Denzell is my best friend. Uncle Moxham met her a score of times at Trengrouse Hall. He used to give her chocolate when she recited her ABCs for him."

Reynolds nodded, smiling, and drifted off to sleep.

That was a strangely vivid memory to have. Katie, her small face solemn but with a glint of fun in her eyes, saying her alphabet for Uncle Moxham. He'd mussed her hair and given her a piece of chocolate, and she'd carefully broken it in three so he and Den could have some too.

Generous to a fault. Always had been.

Somehow, that memory made him uncomfortable. As though he and Den had taken advantage of her; but they'd always shared any treats they had with her and Melissa, and Kerenza too! Katie had always been more…more adaptable than his own sisters, though. He rose from his chair and went to stare out of the window.

Was he taking advantage of her now? He'd tried so hard *not* to, despite his growing awareness of her beauty. He'd refrained physically, thinking he'd give her as much time as she needed, and thought that was enough. But she'd been so unhappy, back at the Hall…he feared he'd let his marriage slide into a kind of habit, where he made no changes to his life, and she made all.

It wasn't fair. Women's lives *weren't* fair. They always had to adapt to their fathers, their husbands, even their sons. That was how things were, but it didn't make it right, any more than slavery in Jamaica was right.

But he was damned if he could figure out what to do about it.

THEY HAD dinner that night in the morning room.

"Since it's just us," Katie explained. As if he'd care.

The food wasn't up to Uncle Moxham's chef's standards, but it was deuced good. Collop of veal in a cream sauce, and a remove of fried salsify, with green beans and roasted beets. And an apple pie to follow.

"That was something like!" He leaned

back and grinned at her. "I didn't know Mrs Barber could cook like that!"

"She can't," Katie said. "I made dinner."

His mouth opened and he knew he was sitting there like a gapeseed, but he couldn't find words.

She ruffled up like a bantam hen. "Don't look so surprised. I do have some household skills."

Damn. He'd offended her.

"It's just—none of my sisters can cook like that!"

Mollified, she relaxed. "Mama believes that if a woman doesn't know all the household arts, her staff will rob her blind."

He hooted with laughter. "I'll lay odds she didn't say 'rob her blind'."

Katie laughed too. "No, she said, 'take advantage of her ignorance. But it was what she meant." She hesitated. "I've ordered Mrs Barber to get extra help from the village to clean this house. I hope that was all right?"

A warmth went through him, surprising him with its strength. "Of course. Of *course* it's all right. This is *your* house too. You're the mistress here."

Strange thought. True, but it conjured up images of a life here, with Katie. Perhaps with a family… She smiled at him as though hearing his thoughts.

"At least until we sell the place," he added. Better not to make promises, even implicit, which he might not want to keep.

Katie's face closed down—perfectly amiable, but no longer warm. "Of course. I'll get it in order so you can sell it."

She rang the bell and rose. "I'll leave you to your port. I'm going to turn in early."

The rustle of her skirt seemed to hang in the air long after she'd gone. He'd made a mess of that. Until he'd looked at the books and ridden over the estate, though, he didn't know *what* he'd be able to do with the place.

Or even what he *wanted* to do. The house was filled with the ghosts of Uncle Moxham and Reynolds in happier days. He wished with all his heart his uncle was here to advise him. About his marriage, about his future, about how to handle being an independent adult...He could almost hear Uncle Moxham's voice saying, "Buck up, lad. Worse things happen at sea!"

Would living here be so bad? It was a long way from home, and family, and most of all from the sea...

He wasn't at all sure he could live away from the sea. Even with Katie.

It wasn't until he was pulling on his nightgown that he realised that "even with Katie" was a thought he'd never had before. He was a married man now, all right.

That didn't make him feel imprisoned quite the way it had before.

There weren't any mounts in the stables except an old nag of Reynolds, so Katie was pleased that they'd brought their own horses along. She walked over to the stableyard wall while she waited for her mare to be brought out.

Autumn mists lay on the flat fields, and

somewhere someone was drying hops; the scent drifted on a slight breeze. It must be the last of the harvest. She loved this season, when fires were lit in every hearth, the mornings were fresh, and the nights began to close in.

"It'll be a fine day once the mist has lifted," Ives said. The groom was waiting, but Ives threw her up and she adjusted her knee between the sidesaddle pommels.

"A lovely day."

He swung up onto his grey gelding and they set off, the groom running to open the first gate for them. She smiled at him and said, "Thank you." Blushing, he tugged his forelock and ducked his head.

"He's not used to women." Ives smiled at her, eyes full of mischief.

"He'll have to get used to me."

There. That was a strong statement of intent. Would Ives pick up on it?

"Perhaps. At some point, I suppose we should talk about the future."

They went in single file down a winding

path and then through another gate (which Ives managed nattily with his riding crop) onto pastureland. As he came up beside her, she took in a breath and said, "Why not talk about it now?"

"It can wait until Reynolds is in the ground, surely?" His tone was harsh; he kicked his horse into a canter and drew away from her.

That wasn't like him. She tapped her mare with her crop and they picked up pace, following Ives. Had she offended him? Or worse, hurt him? He must think her hard-hearted, like a vulture waiting for Reynolds to die.

But it *wasn't* that. She hoped Reynolds recovered and lived for another twenty years! Tears pricked her eyes. She just wanted a home of her own.

Riding next to him, both silent, she cast around for another topic of conversation. But before she could find one, he spoke.

"I'm sorry, my dear. I find...I find I'm missing my uncle quite damnably now I'm back here, and Reynolds' illness… it's hard to imagine the place without either of them."

Her heart broke a little at the pain in his voice. "I understand."

"I know it's not fair to you–" he began.

"We have plenty of time to make decisions. Let's just get through the next few weeks and see where we are."

Sighing with relief, he reined in. Her mare stopped too. Ives reached across and took her hand. Even through her leather gloves she could feel the heat in his hand, and her stomach clenched. He touched her so rarely.

"I think I was very lucky to take you to wife, Kate." He kissed her hand, and then rode on.

He'd always been good at blarney, and no doubt this was more of it. She'd be a fool to see more in it than that. But "Kate". That was new.

She quite liked it.

CHAPTER 9

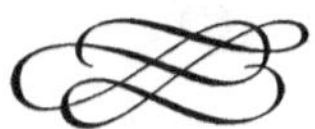

They fell into a pattern: both of them looked after Reynolds, helping his valet Crowley as best they could. In the mornings, once he'd dropped back off to sleep, Ives either went through the books or rode on inspection tours of the estate.

Katie was busy directing the new maids and becoming acquainted with the local gentry.

The ladies from round about had left their cards, but had been kind enough to delay visiting until she'd had time to get the house in order. No doubt they knew from their own servants the state things had been allowed to get into.

Once the house was shining and fresh again, Katie sent a footman around to everyone who had left cards, with cards of her own (kindly supplied by Mr Walton when they'd first married, and never used until now), and the message that she would be "at home" tomorrow.

She waited in the main salon for her first public appearance as Mrs Trengrouse.

Oddly, she wasn't nervous. She knew they'd come, which was the main thing. Sheer curiosity would drive them. And she was her Mama's daughter, drilled in every aspect of polite society. She didn't fear making a misstep.

It was odd, feeling so confident. If Mama had been here, her constant admonitions and complaints would have undermined that, which was something to think about for the future. She was an adult now, a married woman, and her mother had no power over her.

The biggest house in the district was the Merryam estate, and Phoebe, the Dowager Countess, was first to arrive, in a waft of French perfume and floating paisley shawl.

"My dear, welcome to Little Foxbury!" She was a slim, golden-headed woman who didn't look anywhere near old enough to be a dowager—partly because her blue eyes twinkled mischievously.

Katie curtseyed and invited her to sit. "It's kind of you to come." She'd primed Mrs Barber, so she knew that tea would arrive at any moment, but the offer had to be made as though she'd just thought of it. "Would you care for some tea?"

"Of course I would. Now, the biddies will be here soon, so tell me anything scandalous about yourself now, before they come! I'm as secret as the grave, I promise!"

How could one not laugh at that? "I'm afraid the only scandal is that my husband and I eloped."

"Ahah! Trust Ives to avoid the standard,

boring courtship and marriage. That boy has never done the 'done thing' in his life."

Tea arrived, and with it two other women. Not "biddies": Miss Margaret Deveny, a very tall brunette with a perfectly proportioned face, and her step-mother, Lady Deveny, a slight, surprisingly young woman with a charming smile.

Conversation became general, but marriages and engagements and children featured prominently; Miss Deveny was engaged to a John Poulteney, of whom everyone seemed to approve (quite a contrast to how they spoke of Ives), Lady Deveny's youngest was a three-year-old boy, the dowager countess was scheming to marry off her son… it was a *grown-up* conversation, and it gave her confidence, even if the other women skillfully extracted information about her own background at the same time. She and Margaret liked each other; with any luck, she'd found a friend here.

The three stayed the full half-hour, and were followed by Lady Mundford, a fading blonde with assessing eyes, whose conversation was not quite so pleasant but who thawed significantly once she found out that Katie had been Miss Kelynack.

"Ah, the Kelynacks! One of the oldest of our gentry families."

"Yes. We've been in Cornwall since before the Conquest, apparently—but of course that's only family legend."

"My cousin Maria married a Kelynack," Lady Mundford pronounced. "She is quite convinced of the title's antiquity."

Well, she would be, wouldn't she? Katie had met her, and been instructed by Mama to not encourage her encroaching ways.

Delicately, Katie ignored the invitation to discuss Maria Kelynack. "The Trengrouses are very nearly as old a family." Katie poured more tea into Lady Mundford's cup. "And, of course, the Earl is the major landholder in our area."

Take that. Ives might be a junior son, but his family were both richer and better-born than Lord Mundford's; at least, so Mrs

Barber had said when she was giving Katie all the background on their neighbours.

She survived that session, and two more with Lady Shilsbury (the Countess of Norford) and Mrs Birchleigh, who was quite cross to have missed Lady Mundford, since they were, she assured Katie, "Absolutely bosom-bows!"

By the end of the afternoon, she had promised to call on five households, and had declined to attend a luncheon at one, and a picnic at another, "While Mr Reynolds' health is so uncertain."

Mrs Birchleigh had *looked* at her at that. A faint unease gripped her, so she hurried on. "My husband, you know, holds him in great esteem as a boyhood mentor."

"Oh, Ives!" Mrs Birchleigh said, and Lady Shilsbury laughed.

"Such a harum-scarum boy!"

Even after they had gone, and the light in the salon windows had begun to dwindle, Katie sat thinking about that. No one, it seemed, in Cornwall or Little Foxbury, thought much of Ives. They all *liked* him, but rather in the way one liked a puppy.

She couldn't blame Ives for not wanting to stay in a place where he was so thoroughly undervalued. But the life here suited her. A house of her own, a staff to manage, tenants to visit and help, a garden to oversee and a still room to fill…yes. This was the kind of life she could imagine being happy in.

At least the afternoon had established *her* as someone worthwhile. A properly married woman, with a household and staff. And husband… the countess had even complimented her on her cook's shortbread (if only she'd known that Katie was the cook!). Yes. This afternoon had shown her that she *did* have a place in the world, if she was prepared to take it.

She dusted her hands off on her skirt and got up to make the dinner.

IVES SLID an invoice off the ledger as silently as he could with one hand. The other clasped

Reynolds'. The farrier was one of their big costs at this time of year, but surely these numbers couldn't be right?

He turned to ask Reynolds and stopped. What a falling off there had been. Reynolds had been a big man, tall and hearty, with a ruddy complexion. Now he was pale as the sheets under him, thin and fragile, blue veins showing on his closed eyelids. Tears pricked at Ives' own eyes, and he let them fall.

Reynolds' breath slipped in and out almost silently. As the afternoon drew on, Ives simply sat, waiting. It wouldn't be long now. He could hear women's voices in the salon down the hall, so he didn't call Katie. Best not to ruin her day. And he wanted to be here alone with his friend; his family, really. Reynolds had no one else.

He slipped away silently, without even a death rattle, while Ives held his hand.

Ives bowed his head and prayed, tears falling, his body aching under his breastbone; a deep, empty, ache. He should have said more, told Reynolds how much he'd meant, given him the love he deserved. Too late.

The dark was drawing in by the time he lifted his head and dried his eyes. The voices were gone; Katie would be alone.

He wanted her. Needed her soft voice, her compassionate gaze, her understanding. Arranging Reynolds' hands across his chest, he opened the window to let the soul out, and went to find his wife.

KATIE WAS USING a fork to pattern around the edge of the steak and kidney pie when Ives came into the kitchen. She smiled up at him; but he looked grave. Sliding the pie across to Mrs Barber, she wiped her hands down and went over to him.

"Reynolds?"

Ives nodded. "He's gone." His voice trembled. Katie took his hands. If only she could hug him! But they weren't on those terms. Or were they? They had been friends all their lives. She slid her arms around his waist and he enfolded her in his embrace, his head resting on her crown. He was shaking a little, and she held him securely until that went away. Poor lamb.

After a few moments, he drew back and took in a deep breath. Katie nodded to Mrs Barber, who nodded back. They had discussed all the things which would need to be done once death arrived.

Mrs Barber brought out a stack of linen from the butler's pantry and Katie took it.

"Let's go up."

Birth and death were women's work. As the mistress of the house, it was her job to lay Mr Reynolds out for burial. Mrs Barber would follow with hot water and rags. Oddly, she wasn't nervous about this. It wasn't the first time; she had helped her mother lay out her father, and that had been a profound and healing time, allowing her to do one last thing for him.

Ives was silent as they climbed the stairs, but he fumbled for her hand, and she balanced the linen on her other arm to give it to him.

Reynolds looked peaceful, and she was pleased to see that Ives had opened the window. One more thing to do before they began.

"Do you want to give the blessing, or shall I?"

He blinked at her. "The blessing?"

"The Cornish blessing."

"Oh. That's right." He straightened. "Let's do it together."

She put down the linens and, hand in hand, they recited it.

"Deep peace of the Running Wave to you;
Deep peace of the Flowing Air to you;
Deep peace of the Quiet Earth to you;
Deep peace of the Shining Stars to you;
Deep peace of the Son of Peace to you."

Saying the words together felt meaningful; their first important ritual as husband and wife. She squeezed his hand afterward as Mrs Barber bustled in, ewer and bowl in hand.

"Out you go, now, husband," Katie said gently. "This is women's work."

He touched her cheek gently with one finger. "Thank you."

She turned to the sombre task with a strange warmth in her heart.

AFTERWARDS, the local carpenter came to measure for the coffin. He was a chatty man, and he was delighted to get a chance to gossip with the lady of the house.

"Strange it do be to see Mr Ives here as master, missus. Seems no more than a blink o' the eye since he were a harum-scarum boy, stealin' apples and stayin' out 'til all hours blackberryin'."

She was getting quite tired of people talking about Ives the boy. Did no one except her see the man he'd grown into?

"He's the master now, and a good master."

Perhaps her voice had been frosty, because he shot her a quick look and went back to his work.

"No doubt, no doubt," he muttered, head down.

What a termagant she was. "I'm sure he'd be pleased to know his old friends remember his boyhood kindly."

Of course he'd be pleased. He was the easiest of men to get on with. Never a cross word, although his life had been turned upside down. Never a sideways look, never a raised voice. Tears pricked her eyes.

He was so *good*. So kind. She wasn't sure when she had fallen deeply in love with him, but she had, with no chance of it ever being returned. His kindness was that of a big brother to a little sister. Maybe a cousin, if she were lucky. For after all, wasn't that what they had always been? As close as any family.

When he wanted children, perhaps then she could teach him to think of her as a wife first, and Den's little sister a long way second.

Her insides cramped with pain at the thought of such a long wait, but there was nothing for it. A lady never made the first move, even if her heart were breaking.

The carpenter noticed her tears, and coughed. "Ar, he were a grand man, Mr Reynolds. He'll be missed."

Thank God she had a ready excuse for her emotion! "Yes," she agreed. "He'll be sorely missed."

Especially by Ives.

THE FUNERAL WAS VERY WELL ATTENDED, Ives was glad to see. Not the high lords and ladies, but all the tenant farmers, and most of the landowners and suppliers who had had business with Reynolds over the years.

Ewan Moffat, Mrs Barber's brother-in-law, who was steward to Lord Ashbury on the neighbouring property, came up to Ives as the mourners began to leave, a man a few years older than Ives at his side. There was a strong family resemblance.

"Moffat." Ives nodded.

"Mr Trengrouse. This is Albert, my sister's son."

He remembered Bert from his schooldays. A clever, hardworking chap who'd helped out around the estate in his holidays. Mrs Barber's son.

"It used to be Bert, surely!" he said, shaking hands with both men.

"Aye, it did. But I'm in a solicitor's office now, and they prefer Albert."

"It does sound more respectable." They grinned at each other and then sobered, remembering the occasion.

"The thing is," Mr Moffat said, "I thought you might be wanting a new steward, now Mr Reynolds…"

That was a good idea. Ives wasn't sure what he was going to do with Kirwich House and the estate, but he'd need an overseer. He certainly wasn't going to live there year round.

"I've trained him up, you see," Mr Moffat added, "and he'd like something a bit more active than a solicitor's clerk."

"Well, that's good enough for me." Ives offered his hand again to Bert. "Come back with me and we'll discuss terms."

Bert grinned widely, brown eyes gleaming.

"I won't let you down, sir."

"If your uncle has trained you, I'm sure you won't."

All the mourners trooped back to the house. Ives, on his grey, was lost in thought during the ride. What *was* he going to do?

No. What were *they* going to do? He didn't want to make a decision without Kate. It was her life, too, and she deserved to have an equal say. What if he chose wrongly, and made her unhappy? A sudden pang hit him, exactly as though someone had shot him through the heart with a fine needle. He couldn't *bear* to disappoint her.

Oh.

That wasn't good.

Falling in love with her was a very, very bad idea. Love, yes. Of course. They could build a fine marriage on mutual liking and even comfortable love, just as his parents had.

But *in love* was a very different beast. Because it was unrequited. He was sure, positive, that she didn't feel that way about him. He'd barely escaped being thought of as her big brother Right now he was more like a cousin. There was no…no desire in the way she looked at him.

And to try to get her to feel that was wrong. Manipulative. Abusing her trust in him.

He had to squash this new, tender feeling right down. *Right* down! Or it would break him apart every time he looked at her.

The grey sidled and he realised he was gripping the reins so hard his knuckles were white. He leant forward to pat the horse's neck and said aloud, "It's all right," but he wasn't at all sure it would ever be right again.

KATE HAD LAID out a fine spread for nuncheon in the hall. The days were beginning to draw in, and cups of hot soup were welcome, along with the cold collation.

She moved among the tenant farmers with ease. Watching her, it was clear to him that she'd been raised to be one of the high *ton*; no one but a great lady would be so kind and welcoming to all classes, while still keeping a proper decorum and distance from those she didn't know well.

Kate should have married a lord. A duke, even. She was wasted on him.

He *needed* her, and the more he thought about it, the stronger the feeling got.

She could never know. He would wait until she wanted children, and never approach her. It just wasn't fair. Women had no power in a marriage; if he loved her, he had to not touch her. Not show his love except in the most ordinary ways.

Should he let her go? It wasn't too late to have it all annulled, even if he'd have to go off to the Continent afterwards, in disgrace for being not enough of a man to consummate his own marriage.

His heart in him rebelled at that. Not just at the nasty jests which would come his way, but the idea of leaving Kate. They'd built something together. Maybe it wasn't what he truly wanted, but it was *something*.

After they'd all gone home, and he'd had his meeting with Bert Barber, he found Kate in the kitchen, directing the maids she'd hired to make up parcels of left over food to dispense to cottagers on the estate. He'd never have thought of that. She was a wonderful chatelaine.

"Thank you. That was perfect," he said. It was inadequate. He would have given her the whole world if he could. She'd made this horrible, damned day bearable.

Kate smiled up at him and nodded to the stable boy that he could collect the baskets.

"And tell them that the baskets themselves are also gifts, in memory of Mr Reynolds."

"Yes'm."

Mrs Barber nodded her approval. "That's

well done, missus. Ahem…may I ask, will you be staying on now?"

The kitchen fell silent and all eyes turned to him. Not to Kate, but to him. Damn. He was the lord of the manor now. Legally he had been for some time, but now…

"No," he said, surprising himself, as though the decision had been made in some back part of his brain he wasn't aware of. "No, we'll be going to London for the Season. Your son will be taking over as steward. Your brother-in-law has trained him, I hear, and I've put the estate in his hands while we're gone. A probationary period."

Mrs Barber flushed red with delight. And no wonder. This was a serious advancement for her Bert.

Time to take a chance on new blood. There was a limit to how much damage the man could do in three or so months.

Katie had watched all this with surprise on her face. He smiled at her.

"I promised you a London Season, didn't I?"

The smile she gave him back was worth everything. Warmth flooded him; warmth and desire. How beautiful she looked in her blacks! Her pale hair shining, skin like porcelain, the curves of her body more womanly than he remembered.

Perhaps in London… No. He couldn't think that way. It wasn't fair to her.

He left the kitchen abruptly and went to his office, a hard lump under his heart.

CHAPTER 10

Katie had been hearing about London from her mother her whole life. "When you have your London Season…," "In London you'll be able to…," "You need a little town polish, but once you're in London…"

Even her father, before he had died three years ago, had smiled at her and said, "I can just see you at Almack's, the belle of the ball!"

And here she was. In London. During the Season. At Almack's.

Darling Aunt Maria had obtained vouchers for her from Lady Jersey, an old friend. It was really just one big room, with balconies above, and tall windows swathed in rich curtains. The sweet smell of beeswax candles drifted down from the huge chandeliers.

Her throat and stomach were alive with nerves. Thank *God* she wasn't a debutante! The eyes that were on her couldn't blight her prospects. She didn't have to worry about being thought *fast*. That made her laugh inside. Who would have thought, four months ago, on the road to Truro, that she would be *glad* she was married?

Around her, the cream of London Society, all dressed to the nines. She herself was in a new gown; her mother, who had scurried to London as soon as she heard they were planning to visit, had insisted they visit *her* modiste. But where, only a few months ago, they had discussed a London wardrobe of white muslin and pale crepe, now she could choose the stronger colours which were allowed to a young matron. She was dressed in a deeper blue than would have been suitable for her maidenly state, a lovely vibrant blue silk with rich lace trimmings.

It had made her wonder just how rich Ives was. He had come to the modiste out of pure curiosity, he'd said, and hadn't blinked at the exorbitant prices.

She tightened her grip on his arm and he patted her hand.

It wasn't his first time at Almack's, she knew, since he'd done his duty by Melissa during her Season. Even so, arriving in his own party rather than under his father's aegis might have been daunting; but he showed no nerves. He might have been taking a stroll down the main street of Little Foxbury, nodding to acquaintances, raising a hand to wave at friends, stopping now and then to introduce her to old schoolmates.

Going to Eton and Oxford apparently meant that, in any gathering of the *ton*, a young man would find friends.

She envied them. None of the girls attached to the friends (sisters and cousins) were known to her. Their expressions told her a great deal. Cornwall was so very far away! Positively rustic! Despite her fine London dress, she felt very much the country cousin.

And then, across the room, like a lighthouse appearing off a lee shore, there was Margaret Deveny!

"Miss Deveny is here, Ives."

"Excellent! John will be here too, then." They made their way around the area set apart for dancing, where a quadrille was being performed with various degrees of accomplishment. Quadrilles depended *so* much on the other dancers being precise!

Margaret greeted her with pleasure and introduced them to a friend, Miss Maddox, a red-head with curves that put Katie's to shame.

"Where's John?" Ives asked.

A cloud went over Margaret's face. "He's not well."

"The old canker, Meg?" Ives' voice was low and caring. She nodded, eyes downcast. Ives took her hand and squeezed. "I'm sorry."

Katie had never met John Poulteney, but Mrs Barber had told her that the young man suffered from indifferent health. Poor thing. And poor Meg; a canker was more than "indifferent health". It was usually fatal.

"His mother and I brought him up to London to see a new doctor," Margaret explained. "The journey was hard on him, so he's resting. My mother insisted I come out anyway. And he insisted too."

"Quite right!" Ives said. "No need for you to mope around at home when the poor chap just wants to sleep."

He signalled a question with his eyes to Katie and she nodded, though she didn't really understand what he was asking. He smiled brilliantly at her, and then at the others.

"Come on, my dear," he said to Margaret. "A dance will take your mind off your worries."

Oh. *That* had been the question. Of course, she *would* have said yes. It was only kind, and clearly Ives had known Margaret for a long time. All those visits to Kirwich House in his school holidays. But it did give her a pang, seeing her husband lead another woman out to take positions in the dance. Which should have been *her* first dance at Almack's.

"That was kind of Ives," Miss Maddox said. "But we can't stand here like wax dummies!" She gestured with her fan to two young officers standing nearby, and they came gladly over to escort them into the set.

Scots' Greys, Katie thought the uniform was. She was dancing with Lieutenant Stewart, and Miss Maddox with Lieutenant Carstairs. Nice young lads. She felt positively maternal towards them, which was ridiculous! By the colours on their chests, they had fought more than once, including at Waterloo. But they were so fresh-faced and open, holding no emotion back.

For the first time, she realised that Ives was hardly ever like that. One never quite knew what he was thinking. He gave a great impression of the carefree, almost foolish, young man, but he was anything but.

Of course, he held a lot of people's secrets. It was well known that he went out with the smugglers. "Any chance for a night sail!" he'd crowed to Den and her once. Petroc had merely shaken his head, amused. And once, in Swain Cove, Granny Smith had pinched his cheek and told him she needed his help that afternoon. No one had ever *proven* that Granny Smith ran the smugglers, but...Katie wondered what other secrets he knew, and how much of himself he was concealing from her.

He *said* he was happy to be married to her, but was he? She might never know the truth of that.

Occasionally, as the dance moved on, she caught glimpses of Ives and Margaret Deveny in the next set. They were laughing. Margaret was so tall and lithe she could look him almost straight in the eyes.

Katie was suddenly sure she was short

and dumpy and boring, and had to force herself to smile at Lieutenant Stewart.

After the music ended, Ives handed Margaret back to her chaperone, Miss Maddox's aunt, and came to escort Katie off the floor. Lady Jersey drifted past and smiled at them, and then paused. "The next dance is a waltz, I believe. You and your husband should try it."

Katie's heart felt as though it actually swelled, taking up so much space in her chest that she could hardly breathe. She had been *approved*. Even if Lady Jersey was a friend of Aunt Maria's, that wouldn't have caused *this*. This was her own achievement. Given the nod to waltz at Almack's.

Ives didn't seem to understand. "Bit of cheek, isn't it? Telling me to dance with my own wife!"

The music started. A lovely Viennese waltz. She turned to Ives and moved onto the floor. "Don't be silly. She was giving me *permission* to dance it."

"What do you need permission for? You're not a debutante."

"No, but it's my first visit. You wouldn't want me to be thought *fast*, would you? It's bad enough that we eloped!" He frowned. She wanted to reach up and stroke the expression away. "It's all *right*, Ives."

He swung her into the dance, holding her closer than was usually done. Well, they *were* married. "Damn these nosy old biddies." Then he caught her gaze and smiled. "Our first dance as a married couple! Let's show these old witches how it's done!"

They'd danced together before, of course. Balls and impromptu hops at picnics on the terrace, with the library windows open so Demelza could play for them. Those had all been country dances. Ives had never held her like this, body to body, his hand strong on her waist, their other hands clasping, the contact warm and disturbing.

Whirling across the floor, they laughed together. It was delightful. Heady, intoxicating, sheer *fun*. It ended too soon, but she was still breathless.

"You're good at this." Her heart leapt. How pitiful that his approval on such a small matter meant so much to her!

WHEN THEY RETURNED to Trengrouse House in Grosvenor Square, there was chaos. The earl and countess had arrived, complete with Locryn, Elestryn, Kerenza, and Felix—and their children and servants. Lion had come up months ago, but was in his own bachelor quarters in Half Moon Street.

His mother was in her customary sergeant major mode, directing the servants as to where to put all the luggage. She greeted Ives and Katie with distracted embraces.

"I'm sorry, Katie, but I've had your Susan move your things into Ives' room. With all the children here, we're full to the rafters!"

"Of course, Aunt Maria," Kate said, but she looked up at him with doubt. Did she think he'd make a scene? What tosh. Sooner or later they would have had to share a room—house parties, visits to friends in less comfortable circumstances…he just had to ignore the feeling that he was burning from the inside out.

"We'll be snug as a bug in a rug," he said. "What do you want us to do now, Mama?"

"Just get out of my way, dear."

"That we can do. But tomorrow you must hear how Katie made a smash at Almack's!"

They escaped up the stairs to Ives' room, where Susan and Neale appeared to be getting on entirely too well. They were laughing together by the window as the door opened, but dove for pieces of clothing and bustled to put them in drawers. Ives raised an eyebrow at his valet, who looked anywhere but at him, and Susan blushed and disappeared into the dressing room.

Katie almost laughed, but bit it back. No need to antagonise her own maid…and good for Susan, if she was lucky in love. Although, it would be unusual for her and Neale to marry; upper servants rarely did. She wasn't quite sure if a lady's maid could be a mother and still work…

Which was sad, now she came to think of it.

She followed Susan into the dressing room; when married people shared a room, usually it was the man who undressed in there, but this *was* Ives' room. She didn't want to be encroaching.

Outside, the night was dark and the wind was rising, but even the dressing room was warm. According to Susan, who talked rapidly while she was undressing Katie and taking her hair down, it was because of an ingenious new system of chimneys and flues which warmed the whole house—"even the attics, madam!" Katie clamped her lips together to stop herself from saying, "Who cares! I'm going to sleep with my husband!"

"There, madam!" Susan finished, standing back. "Now you're ready for Mr Ives."

The woman who looked back at her from

the dressing room mirror didn't look ready for anything. She looked far too young and gauche to be a married woman with a husband waiting for her in the next room. What if Ives…?

Well, what if he did? Wasn't it *time*? She was tired of this half-life; not quite a maiden, not quite a wife. He might not love her, but surely he could, could *make* love to her? Men didn't mind not having love in the bedroom, did they? Her mother had always said not.

And apart from anything else (like Ives' long, beautiful hand warm on her waist as they waltzed), she'd quite like to have a baby. At least, she thought she would. It was certainly expected of her. There had been more than one assessing look at her waistline from the chaperones' corner tonight.

Susan had put her in one of her trousseau nightgowns, which Mama had insisted upon her buying, well before the Trengrouse ball. She was glad now. The cream lace and pale pink silk made her skin glow. Or perhaps that was the blush which fought to take her over.

"Thank you, Susan." Their eyes met in the mirror, and Susan smiled.

Impossible to say aloud what they were thinking, but there was a good deal of encouragement in that smile. Of course Susan knew the truth of her marriage. Servants always knew everything.

Hesitantly, she pushed open the door to the bedroom. Neale had gone, thank goodness. There was a candle on each of the nightstands by the bed, leaving the bed in overlapping circles of light, the peacock-blue bed curtains shining. Ives was lying down on the far side, his nightshirt-clad back to her. She approached slowly. Should she go around to his side, or get in at hers?

Courage failing, she slid into her side of the bed, conscious with each movement of how close she was getting to him. She could feel the warmth coming off his back.

"Ives…"

Nothing.

"Ives?"

The damn man was *asleep*! Asleep! Oh, that was just–

Katie picked up a pillow and smashed him over the head with it.

He bolted up and looked around wildly, and she caught him another buffet, right in the face.

"How *dare* you go to sleep! This is our first night together since our wedding night, and you fall *asleep*?" She pulled the pillow back for another blow, but he caught it and pulled it from her grasp, holding it before him like a shield.

"I *wasn't* asleep! I was *pretending*! To make it easier on you!"

They sat for a moment in silence, staring at each other, both breathing hard.

"Oh," she said.

Suddenly that seemed very funny. They both burst out laughing; so hard that they had to lean against each other for support. Ives let the pillow fall to the floor. Tears crept out of Katie's eyes, and she wiped them away with her sleeve, hiccupping for breath.

As the laughter died away, something else grew. Their heads were together, her forehead on his shoulder. He smelled of lime and musk. The lime was the soap Aunt Maria preferred to buy. The musk was all him.

His hand touched her chin, and she raised her head. His face was troubled.

"I've tried to give you time…" His voice was uncertain. "But, if you…if you might want children…"

Children were not the first reason that came to mind. But could she tell him the truth, that she wanted *him*? Her whole body threatened to turn to hot liquid, just sitting like this next to him. What could she say that wouldn't sound forward? Her mother had been so *clear* that she was never to make the first move.

"I'm…I'm just tired of not being *really* married," she said. "I don't feel properly *adult*."

Laughter lit his eyes again, and something else. Was that desire? "I suppose that makes sense. But we will be risking children, Kate. Are you ready for that?"

Had she thought of children earlier because everyone expected her to want them? But there was no reason *not* to have children. And she quite liked babies.

"I think so."

"Better to be sure." She couldn't tell him she was sure she desired him. If Ives thought badly of her, it would be crushing. She couldn't risk that.

"Yes. Yes. I want to be a proper wife and mother." That was clear enough, surely? Even Mama couldn't disapprove of that.

"Well then…" He bent to kiss her.

Her first kiss that wasn't under a quick peck under the mistletoe.

His mouth was soft on hers; her whole body flared into urgent life.

OH, how he'd wanted this!

Not just Kate's mouth beneath his, her body soft in his arms, but *her* wanting it too!

He was overwhelmed with tenderness.

The softness of her mouth, the trust she put in him, the rose scent rising from her skin…he was drunk on her.

Dare he tell her how he felt? No doubt but that this was love. Once he'd said the word, there was no going back.

He kissed down the side of her neck and felt her shiver with pleasure. His own body leapt in response.

Love could be left until later. This would do for now…

He would do what the marriage vows said, and worship her with his body.

CHAPTER 11

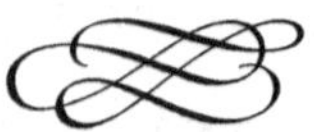

hey were both shy over their morning chocolate, which Susan brought with an indulgent smile on her face.

Katie felt rather as she had when they'd visited Brighton a few years ago and she'd been "dipped" by a large, muscular woman who had pushed her up and down vigorously in the sea and swished her around as though she weighed no more than a baby.

Every muscle had come alive then and had stayed strangely warm for some time afterward.

So it was now. Each part of her body felt

simultaneously languorous and full of energy, as though the memory of the extraordinary pleasure she'd experienced was seared into her very flesh.

She risked a glance at Ives, who looked at her with unexpected tenderness. Or, was it unexpected? He had treated her with such consideration… "trust your husband". For once, Mama had been entirely right. She could trust Ives with her life.

A warm bubble of emotion filled her. This was love. She was sure of it now. He was so *kind*. But more than that, so genuinely thoughtful, and gentle, and yet so strong. How had she ever believed him thoughtless and casual?

Wordlessly, she put out her hand and took his. His smile broke over his face like a sunrise. He lifted her hand and kissed her knuckles, and her entire body remembered his in a rush of heat.

So kind. So loving…but he had not said he loved her. And what had happened last night might be how it always was between husband and wife. That seemed unlikely, somehow, but it could be true. How would she know? She shouldn't assume it *meant* anything.

Neale appeared with Ives' shaving water as they finished their chocolate, and the day took on its accustomed shape. A day like any other day.

But she would never be the same again.

CHAPTER 12

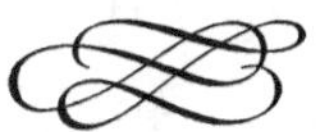

'Mr Ives, a message for you.' Their butler, Mr Carveth, whom Mama had brought to Town with her, proffered a note on a salver. He nodded his thanks. It must be important, for Carveth to have interrupted breakfast.

A letter from Tom Moffat. Ives read it and felt his stomach drop into a pit.

"What is it? Is everything all right?" Kate asked. The rest of the family looked up in curiosity. Including Lady Kelynack, who'd been invited for breakfast so she could join them on a picnic excursion to Richmond.

"It's from Kirwich. Albert Barber has absconded with the quarter's wages and some silver from the house."

A babble of voices broke out as Kate took his hand and squeezed it.

"Poor Mrs Barber! She must be crushed."

"Typical Ives," Demelza said. "Rushed into it as usual and paying the price."

"Oh, Ives!" his mother sighed. "Really, you should be more careful."

"This is why you need to come to me for advice before you make these kinds of decisions, boy!" His father shook his head. "You should have thoroughly checked this man's credentials before you hired him."

"You're a married man now, Ives," Lady Kelynack admonished him. "You must grow up and take on adult responsibilities!"

He could feel the weight of their disappointment—the sense that he had never been good enough, never *would* be good enough to please them—bear down on him like a heavy weight.

Kate stood up abruptly. "You should all be quiet!" Astonished, they were silent. Except for Kate's Mama, who began to speak.

But Kate held up her hand, although it shook a little. "No, Mama. Let me speak." She took in a deep breath. She looked straight at his father, who stared back in a mixture of surprise and anger. "Lord Trengrouse, Ives *did* check his credentials. He was recommended by a local steward who runs Lord Ashbury's estate, and by the solicitors he worked for. *And* he was the son of my housekeeper."

My housekeeper. His chest began to fill with warmth. She was putting herself right in the middle of it, for him.

"And the rest of you! You treat him as though he's five years old. Have *any* of you talked to Mr Walton about how capable he is? Have any of you even *looked* at him in the last few years? It's always, 'Oh, it's only Ives!' Even when we got *married* you treated it like a prank!"

His Mama opened her mouth, but Demelza put her hand out to stop her speaking. Lady Kelynack wasn't to be deterred.

"I understand you have a partiality for him, my dear, but you can't deny that he's a thoughtless, scapegrace young rapscallion!" She finished with a satisfied smile, sure that Kate would wither and back down, as she always did when her mother overbore her.

He wanted to slap her across her domineering face. But this was Kate's battle. He slid his hand across so that his fingers touched hers where they rested on the table's edge.

KATIE FELT the pressure to give in, as she always did, but this was *Ives* who was being traduced. She couldn't let him down. She felt his fingers touch hers, and drew strength from it. "I *can* deny it, and I do! He's a responsible landholder, a kind, thoughtful, *wonderful* husband, and I will *not* allow you to insult him."

Silence reigned as she locked gazes with her mother. Incredibly, Mama looked aside first. But then she looked back.

"Katherine, I do think this behaviour is unbecoming. To speak like a fishwife to your papa-in-law–" She drew breath, and Ives cut in.

"My father would prefer his family spoke the truth to him. Wouldn't you, Papa?"

Back him up. Just this once. Just once. Katie prayed.

"I don't appreciate being contradicted in my own house by a chit of a girl–" the earl began.

"My *wife*, sir. And you will speak of her with respect. Or we leave this house within the hour."

Ives stood so he was shoulder to shoulder with her. To stand up to his father, for *her*. That was real anger in his voice, as though he *cared*. She was overcome with the certainty that he loved her. It was as though she'd been falling, without anything to catch onto, for *months*, ever since the Trengrouse Ball, and now he was there, holding her fast.

The earl looked at him curiously, as though seeing him for the first time, a small curl at the corner of his mouth suggesting he wasn't displeased by this rebellion.

"Hoity-toity, are you?" He nodded at Ives to go on. "What else do you have to say for yourself?"

"Ives," she whispered. She didn't want to be the cause of problems between him and his father. He took her hand.

"My wife is right. I did check Barber's credentials thoroughly, and he was of good repute. I can only assume his circumstances changed. I have known him most of my life, Papa. He wasn't some fly-by-night I found by the side of the road. In any case, the error was mine, and the price will be paid by me. And let's not forget that we're talking about a sum less than I pay for one of Kate's beautiful gowns."

This reminder allowed them all to relax a little, even the Earl.

"I suppose no lasting harm has been done," he admitted.

The family went on with their breakfast as though nothing had happened, with only Lady Kelynack still glaring at them. For the first time ever, Katie could ignore her.

"Except to Mrs Barber," Katie said. "We'd best go to Kirwich immediately, Ives, and make sure she knows she still has a position."

"Yes, we need to set things to right there, but I can go myself. I don't want to interrupt your Season."

She smiled up at him. "There'll be other Seasons. I want to be with *you*."

He couldn't kiss her, not here, not now. But she could tell he wanted to, and it warmed her to tips of her toes.

"We'll pack and be on our way to Kirwich then, Mama. Papa."

"I'm not going to apologise, if that's what you want–" the earl began.

"No, Papa, it's not that. But I have to get back to arrange things, and Kate wants to go with me."

"Young love," the earl said, shaking his head.

"Yes," Kate said. She gripped Ives' hand hard. There was no going back now. She had to take however he responded and live with it.

"That's us," he said, squeezing her hand in return, and her heart shot up, a fountain of delight and joy. And desire.

She looked up at him, trying to put all she felt in her eyes, and he trembled.

He loved her. They had come so close to alienating both their families, but miraculously had skated through, and now he loved her.

They raced upstairs hand in hand, as they might have done when they were children. At the top of the stairs he pulled her into an embrace and kissed her with fully adult desire.

She slid her arms around his neck and curved her body into his. Home. This was home. Perhaps they'd stay at Kirwich, perhaps they'd sell it and buy somewhere in

Cornwall. Perhaps they'd go sailing the seven seas.

It didn't matter. Wherever he was, she was where she wanted to be.

HE RAISED his head and gazed down at Kate's beautiful face.

"Is it very bad of me to hope you don't get with child just yet?" he asked. His thumb stroked her cheek. "I'd rather like a honeymoon. A real one, this time."

"I'd like that too."

"Then let's go home, wife. Home for now, at least. You can decide where we're going to live permanently later."

"As long as it's near the sea?"

Ives laughed. "You know me too well!"

Kate kissed him. Now she knew he loved her, it was clear that Mama's advice about never making the first move was absolute nonsense.

"I know you enough to love you."

He stilled, and then kissed her back, a long, lingering, beautiful kiss.

"Beloved," he said. There was a little catch in his voice which almost broke her heart.

"Always," she said.

"Let's go home."

They went into the bedroom hand in hand, united.

The Cornish Blessing is more properly called a Celtic blessing, but it has been found on the walls of Cornish churches, so I've appropriated it here.

MORE FROM ELIZABETH LEYDIN

I hope you've enjoyed the second book in the Trengrouse Ball series. There are more–see below.

Sign up for Elizabeth's Substack blog, 'Corsets & Coaches', where she shares true-life Regency stories and tidbits, as well as news about her latest releases, or watch her "This Week in the Regency" videos on Youtube.

More Trengrouse Ball Sweet Regency Romances

The Trengrouse Ball books can all be read as stand-alones – the timelines overlap, but each story is separate.

The Captain and the Lady
Book 1 in the Trengrouse Ball series

Petroc Trengrouse has come home from Waterloo missing his right leg.

Family friend Lady Beatrice Marlowe has been thrown out of her home on the deaths of her father and brother.

When Petroc comes to stay at Beatrice's mother's seaside house to recover from his wounds, he has no idea that he's causing severe financial problems.

He feels he's not fit to marry; she knows she's too poor to attract an aristocratic suitor. Will the Trengrouse Ball prove both of them wrong?

Second Chance at Christmas
Book 3 in the Trengrouse Ball series

A heart-warming second chance Christmas story.

Widowed, pregnant Lady Demelza Mandeville returns to her family home, Trengrouse Hall, after her husband's recent death, dreading meeting family friend, Sir Denzell Kelynack, who jilted her in her first Season.

Denzell looks forward to the meeting—he wants to know why Demelza had jilted him eight years ago. And what role did his needy, unstable mother play in that?

Finding out the truth, and finding a path to a new life, is complicated by Demelza's pregnancy. If the baby is a boy, she'll be bound to the Mandeville estates until he's an adult; if a girl, she's free to live her own life while a Mandeville cousin inherits the estate.

The Trengrouse Ball is a promise of things to come, but will the promise come true at Christmas?

The Baboon at the Ball
Book 4 in the Trengrouse Ball series

A forbidden love story with animal antics to upset the normal order of things! (Or, a Cinderella story with a difference…)

Val Muffet is a Cit—a rich, well-educated, beautifully-mannered man, but definitely *not* one of the *ton,* despite being invited to the Trengrouse Ball.

Lady Kerenza Trengrouse's family is amongst the great and the good of the land, and she expects to marry a lord. An earl, at least!

What could bring these two to care about each other? Enter Genevieve, the lost, forlorn but definitely challenging baboon, given to the Muffets by the Prince Regent himself.

Genevieve is *not* invited to the ball, but she comes anyway, and life will never be the same again for Val or Kerenza!

This story was first published in The Regent's Menagerie, Volume 1.

My Earl, the Spy
Book 5 in the Trengrouse Ball series

An exciting ace romance with a twist of espionage!

Lady Melissa Trengrouse can't imagine being married to anyone but Charles Goddard, Earl of Westholm, for whom she decodes secret French dispatches.

Although she hates the idea of marriage or children, for Charles, Melissa would endure it all. They're perfect for each other: but when she proposes to him at the Trengrouse Ball, he refuses her without explanation.

Charles has his reasons. He hates hurting her, but it's a relief when he has to ride off on a secret mission for the Crown.

Melissa realises he's riding into a trap. Can she save him and discover his secret reasons for denying that he loved her all along?

A sweet Regency romance with an atypical couple!

The Lion and Miss Lamb
Book 6 in the Trengrouse Ball series

Sarah Lamb doesn't have a family; Endellion Trengrouse has never fit in with his.

Immediately attracted, the two have a brief flirtation at the Trengrouse Ball, which ends disastrously when Endellion—known as Lion—finds out the truth behind Sarah's birth. Sarah isn't surprised by his reaction: she knows no respectable man will marry an illegitimate orphan.

But there's more to Sarah's parentage—and Endellion's—than either of them know. Can they find the truth…and will that truth bring them together, or drive them apart?

This story first appeared in the Sweet Daughters of Duke Street series.

www.ingramcontent.com/pod-product-compliance
Lightning Source LLC
Chambersburg PA
CBHW071013180726
48291CB00004B/1437